The Green Story Book

This is the fourth
in Enid Blyton's series
of 'Colour' books for
young readers

Published by Granada Publishing Limited
in Dragon Books 1967
Reprinted 1969, 1971, 1974, 1976, 1979

ISBN 0 583 30025 1

First published in Great Britain
by Methuen & Co Ltd 1947
Copyright © Enid Blyton 1947

Granada Publishing Limited
Frogmore, St Albans, Herts AL2 2NF
and
3 Upper James Street, London W1R 4BP
1221 Avenue of the Americas, New York, NY 10020, USA
117 York Street, Sydney, NSW 2000, Australia
100 Skyway Avenue, Toronto, Ontario, Canada M9W 3A6
110 Northpark Centre, 2193 Johannesburg, South Africa
CML Centre, Queen & Wyndham, Auckland 1, New Zealand

Made and printed in Great Britain by
C. Nicholls & Company Ltd
The Philips Park Press, Manchester
Set in Monotype Plantin

Granada Publishing ®

Enid Blyton

The Green Story Book

Text Drawings by Jenny Chapple

DRAGON
GRANADA PUBLISHING
London Toronto Sydney New York

'That's the Land of Nod,' whispered the old woman

The Bed That Ran Away

Once upon a time there was a small girl called Anna and a small boy called Guy. Guy was a wide-awake little fellow, but Anna – dear me, *what* a sleepy-head she was!

She would *not* wake up in the morning! She was always yawning all the day long, and she was always ready to go to bed at night.

Her mother used to get very tired of trying to wake her up each morning. She would go into Anna's room and say: "Anna. Wake up! Time to get up!"

No answer from Anna.

"ANNA! WAKE UP! YOU'LL BE LATE FOR SCHOOL!"

"M-mm-m-mm!" Anna would mumble, half asleep. Her mother would pull all the clothes from her bed and cry, "You lazy little girl! Get up, I say!"

Then she would go from the room – and that lazy little Anna would pull up the clothes again and go to sleep once more! So she hardly ever had time for a proper breakfast, and was always late for school.

One day her mother was so cross that she said she couldn't be bothered to wake up Anna any more.

"You shall wake her up, Guy," she said. "Do what you like – squeeze a cold sponge over her – take off the blankets and put them on the other side of the room – but wake her up!"

So Guy said he would – but, dear me, it *was* difficult, because Anna could sleep even though cold water was pouring over her face, and when she found that her bed-clothes were on the other side of the room, why, she just went to sleep again without them, curling up her toes inside her night-dress for warmth. She *was* a sleepy-head!

Now one of Guy's school-fellows had an old grandmother who was supposed to be a very wise woman. She often went out in the early mornings and picked queer herbs and strange leaves to make potions. She was a kindly old woman, always ready to help anyone, and Guy wondered if she would be able to tell him how to cure Anna of her sleepiness.

So one evening he went to call on her. She lived in a little cottage on the edge of the wood. The old dame opened the door herself and smiled at Guy.

"Hallo, little man, and what can I do for you?" she asked.

Guy told her his trouble and she listened with a twinkle in her eye.

"A sleepy-headed sister!" she said, when he had finished. "Well, we must certainly cure her, Guy, or she won't be a bit of use in the world."

"Can you cure her?" asked Guy eagerly.

"I'm not quite sure," said the old woman. She went to a drawer and opened it. In it were the queerest things Guy had ever seen – peacocks' feathers, sparkling powders, small dolls like pixies, shining butterflies' wings neatly piled together, and tiny bottles of bright-coloured liquids.

The old dame took out a small yellow box and opened it. Inside were a number of very tiny shining stars, glittering brightly.

The old woman shook three out into her hand. "Now these," she said, "are supposed to be a sure cure for a sleepy-head. Put one under the sleepy person's pillow and it is said he will be cured by the next day. If not, put a second under his pillow the next night and a third the following night. After that he will wake up early every morning and never be a sleepy-head again. But these little stars are very old and may have lost their powers, so don't trust too much to them, Guy. You can try them if you like."

"Oh, thank you!" cried Guy. He took an empty match-box from his pocket and slipped inside it the three curious stars. They shone strangely and seemed full of magic.

"What do they do, to make the sleepy-head wake up?" he asked.

"Oh, it is said that the bed makes a curious creaking noise, which so much frightens the person in bed that he wakes up at once!" said the old dame. "You must watch and see what happens, Guy!"

Guy said good-bye and thank you, and ran home. What a secret he had! He took out the stars and looked at them. Would they really be powerful enough to cure such a sleepy person as Anna? Surely a little creaking and groaning wouldn't wake her up!

"I think I shall put all three stars under her pillow," decided the little boy. "Then perhaps the bed will make such a loud noise that it will waken even Anna!"

So that night when Anna was fast asleep in bed, Guy stole up to her and slipped all three of the little shining stars under her pillow. Then off he went to his own bed, and left his door open so that he could hear when Anna's bed began to creak and groan.

At five o'clock in the morning, when the sun was just rising and all the world was golden, Guy woke up. Whatever was all that noise? He sat up in bed and remembered. Ah, it was Anna's bed! How angry she would be to be wakened up at five o'clock.

He slipped out of his bed and ran into Anna's bedroom. The little girl was lying fast asleep as usual, but the bed was behaving very queerly!

It groaned deeply. It creaked heavily. It tossed the mattress up and down as if it were trying to shake Anna out of bed. But she didn't move!

Guy stood and watched. It was very strange to see. Then he saw something even stranger!

The bed lifted up one foot and pawed the floor with it like a horse! Guy didn't like that much. It was too strange. Whatever would it do next?

It lifted up another foot and knocked on the floor with that too – and then, oh my goodness me, it began to move! Yes, it really did! It walked towards the door, creaking and groaning for all it was worth, putting out first one foot and then another, just as if it were a four-legged animal!

Guy tried to push the bed back into its place, but it tapped him smartly on the toe and made him jump. It pushed him away and squeezed itself through the door. And then it jolted itself down the stairs! It made such a noise all the time, creaking like a dozen doors and grumbling to itself like a live thing! Guy didn't know *what* to do!

"Anna, Anna, wake up!" he cried. "Your bed is walking away with you!"

"Mm-m-mm-m-mm!" said Anna in her sleep.

"Anna! Get up!" shouted Guy, trying to roll the little girl out of bed. But she only curled herself up all the more tightly and slept soundly. It was quite impossible to waken her.

Guy was just going to run and waken his parents when he saw the bed was beginning to run! It had got down the stairs and somehow or other the front door had opened and now the bed was out in the street, running merrily! There was no time to get help. By the time he had wakened his mother the bed would be out of sight and nobody would know where Anna had gone! He must keep close to the bed, whatever happened. If only he could wake Anna!

The bed jogged on happily, creaking as it went. Guy ran after it, still in his sleeping-suit, for he had had no time to dress. It ran faster. Guy ran fast too. The bed made for a little lane and rushed down it, almost galloping, so that Anna was jolted up and down, but still she didn't wake! Guy tore after the bed. It turned a corner and Guy ran to the corner, too – but when he got there, the bed was gone!

"It's gone!" said Guy, in horror. "Where is it?"

There was no bed to be seen. It had vanished into thin air. Not a creak, not a groan was to be heard. Poor Guy! Tears came into his eyes but he dashed them away. Crying wouldn't help Anna! No, he must go straight to the old woman who had given him those little shining stars and see if she could tell him where the bed had gone.

So off he went to the old dame, and she was most surprised to have such an early visitor. When she heard what had happened she sat down in amazement.

"You shouldn't have put all three stars under the pillow," she said at last. "Of course that would give the bed power to run straight away! One star just makes it want to go, and it creaks and groans because it can't – but three stars! Well, of course it would disappear!"

"But Anna didn't wake up," said Guy in despair.

"She *must* be a sleepy-head!" said the old dame. "Well, well, we must see what we can do. The bed has gone to the Land of Nod, you know. Perhaps if we go there we can manage to rescue Anna."

"Oh, will you go with me?" asked Guy.

"Of course!" said the old dame. "Come and sit on my knee in my big arm-chair and it will take us to the Land of Nod, where we can look for poor Anna."

She sat down, and Guy climbed up on to her knee.

She began to tell him a story. It was a sleepy story, and Guy, who was tired, gradually felt his head beginning to nod. He would soon be asleep. The chair began to rock, for it was a rocking-chair. It rocked and rocked so hard that Guy opened his eyes in surprise.

And do you know, it wasn't a chair after all! It was a boat, rocking on a deep blue sea. He was sitting on a soft cushion and the old dame was opposite him, smiling broadly.

"Well, we are on the way to the Land of Nod," she said. "We shan't be long in this boat."

The sea stretched for ever around them – or so it seemed. No land was in sight anywhere. Fish gleamed in the depths of the blue water, like stars. Guy wished he could catch some.

"We're nearly there," said the old woman.

"Where?" asked Guy, in surprise. He could see nothing at all but sea!

And then to his enormous surprise, a curious cloudy land seemed to rise out of the blue sea just by him. It grew bigger and bigger, its towers shot up to the clouds, its palaces glimmered in the pale sunshine.

"That's the Land of Nod," whispered the old woman. "You mustn't make a noise here in case you wake the sleepers."

"Who are they?" asked Guy.

"Oh, I expect Anna is one of them by now!" said the old dame, with a laugh.

The boat came softly to shore. The old dame got out and helped Guy to land. There was no wind, not a sound of any sort to be heard.

"It's just like a dream!" said Guy, in a whisper.

"Well, you can only come here in a dream, you know," said the old woman. "Now we must see if we can find

Anna." Nobody was in the blue, misty streets. Guy's slippers seemed to make such a noise in that silent land.

Suddenly a white rabbit appeared, his long ears twitching forwards. When he saw Guy and the old woman he ran silently towards them.

"Take off your shoes," he hissed. "Don't you know that if you wake anyone in the Land of Nod a nightmare will gallop up and carry you away and you'll never be seen again?"

"Ooh!" said Guy in a fright. He took off his shoes at once. He didn't want to be galloped off on the back of a night-mare!

The rabbit disappeared. The old woman pointed silently to a big palace not far off.

"That's where the sleepers are!" she whispered. "Come on!"

They made their way to the palace. Its many pinnacles shone silvery in the early morning light. There was a great flight of steps up to a wide, glass door.

The little boy and the old woman went softly up and just as they reached the top a sound came to their ears! It came from behind them. They turned to look.

And whatever *do* you think they saw? Why, Anna's bed coming slowly up the steps! Yes, they had got to the Land of Nod first!

The bed creaking softly, and groaning under its breath, came up the steps one foot after another – and Anna still lay there, fast asleep! Would you believe it!

The bed pushed open the glass door and went inside. The other two followed. What a queer sight met their eyes in the palace!

There was a long hall and on either side were beds – some big, some small, but all with sleepers in, curled up in slumber. Anna's bed wandered down the hall, as if it were

11

looking for a place. There was none for it, so it went through another door and into a smaller room. Beds were here too, but still there was no room! Into yet another room went the bed, groaning to itself as if it were very tired.

In this third room there was a space big enough for one more bed. Anna's bed walked carefully backwards into it and then, with a soft creak of delight, stood perfectly still. It had found its place in the Land of Nod!

"How can we wake her?" asked Guy, in a whisper.

"You can't!" said the old woman. "Nobody does anything but sleep here. We shall have to do the only thing we can – make the bed take her back home again!"

"But how can we do that?" asked Guy, in surprise.

"If you can manage to take away the three little stars you put under Anna's pillow, I think the bed will have to go back," said the old dame. "It hasn't got rooted here yet, as all the others have! It has only just come. But I'm afraid it will be very angry!"

Guy went to stand beside the bed. He put his hand under Anna's pillow and felt about for the three little stars. It really seemed as if they didn't want to be taken away for they ran about under the pillow like live things, and pricked Guy's hand whenever they could. But at last he got hold of them, slipped them into his match-box and gave them to the old woman.

"Not we'll see what happens!" said the old dame. "Stand back a little!"

As soon as the bed knew that the little magic stars were gone, it began to make a terrible noise, for it knew it would have to go back to where it came from. It began to creak as loudly as twenty wardrobes, and groaned so deeply that even Guy jumped. Then it moved! First one foot and then the other, but what a noise it made! It knocked here, it stamped there, it even seemed to dance with rage. Anna

12

was shaken up and down but she didn't wake up! The bed moved out of its corner and went down the room. It ran out of the door, stamping and creaking like a mad thing.

And then suddenly the palace was full of strange horses with gleaming eyes and long tails. The night-mares had come! They stamped their hooves, and raced about in anger, and Guy felt frightened of them. He began to climb up on a bed where a sleeper lay, lost in slumber – but the old woman pulled him off at once.

"You'll never go back home if you get into one of these beds!" said she.' 'The only thing to do is to catch a night-mare and ride it. It will take you home all right, though it will not be a pleasant ride!"

Guy did as he was told. He ran to one of the prancing coal-black night-mares and clambered on to its back. It threw up its head, made a whinnying noise and then galloped off at top speed. Guy clung on for all he was worth.

It was not at all a nice ride, as the old woman had said. The horse seemed to delight in giving poor Guy as many frights as it could. It galloped into a moonlit land, and came to a high cliff. Far down below was the gleaming sea. The mare, instead of stopping at the edge of the cliff, jumped right over it! Guy gave a gasp. Whatever would happen? Would they fall into the sea? But no! The horse grew a pair of wings in mid-air and flapped safely back to the cliff-edge, with Guy clinging tightly to its neck. It hrrumphed in delight when it saw how frightened Guy was.

Off it galloped again, and this time Guy saw a great wall in front of them. Surely, surely, the mare was not going to try and jump that! She would never get over the top!

But the horse gave a spring and up it went, with Guy wondering whatever would be on the other side. Over the top of the wall they went and then Guy saw a swiftly flow-ing river on the far side of the wall. Splash! Into it they went, and the mare began to swim. Two or three times waves splashed over Guy's shoulders and he swallowed some water.

The night-mare scrambled out the other side and gal-loped off again with Guy almost tumbling off. It went so fast that the little boy's hair streamed out in the wind. Faster and faster – faster and faster and faster! Guy clung on tightly. Goodness, surely the horse couldn't go *much* faster!

Suddenly the animal put its hoof into a rabbit-hole and over it went. Guy shot up into the air and came down again – bump!

He gasped and opened his eyes.

And will you believe it, he was at home! By him was his bed, and he was on the floor.

"Well, anyone would think I had fallen out of bed!" he thought, getting up. "Anyway, I'm safely back from the Land of Nod – but what about Anna?"

He ran to his sister's room – and was just in time to see the bed squeezing itself in at the door again, creaking and groaning! Anna was fast asleep, of course! The bed went to its place and stood perfectly still and silent. A clock downstairs struck seven.

His mother came out of her room.

"Hallo, Guy," she said. "Do try to get Anna down in time for breakfast today."

Guy woke Anna by pulling her out of bed and making her go bump on the floor. Then he sat down by her and told her all the exciting adventures of that morning, and how she had been to the Land of Nod and back.

"Oh!" said Anna, turning pale. "Do you know, I dreamt it, too! I knew everything that happened, but I

14

couldn't wake up. Oh! Guy, just suppose I'd stayed there! "

"Well, if I were you I'd get up each morning as soon as you are called," said Guy, "just in case that bed of yours starts off again! "

"Oh, I will! " said Anna, and dressed in a hurry, anxious to get away from her queer bed. How surprised her mother was to see her down to breakfast ten minutes early!

The next morning, whilst Anna was still asleep, the bed creaked a little. My goodness, you should have seen Anna! She sat up in bed at once, leapt out and dressed as quickly as she could – and that bed has only got to give the smallest creak each day for Anna to be up and dressing in two shakes of a duck's tail!

"I'm not going to be taken off to the Land of Nod again! " she says – and I'm not surprised, are you?

The Boy Who Was Afraid

Once upon a time there was a little boy called Mark who didn't like going to the seaside. This was very queer of him, because the seaside is a lovely place, with sands to play on and water to paddle in.

But Mark was afraid of the sea. It looked so big to him, and it was wet and cold. He didn't like the big waves that rolled up the sand and curled round his ankles. He was afraid they would take him back to the sea with them.

His Daddy and Mummy were ashamed of him, because he screamed whenever they wanted him to put on his bathing-suit and go bathing with them. He wouldn't even paddle in the sea. The only thing he would do was to wade in the warm little pools that the tide left among the rocks when it went out.

One very warm sunny day, his Mummy and Daddy went into their tent to put on their bathing-suits to go into the water. Mark felt sure he would have to put on his suit too, and he was afraid. So he made up his mind to run away whilst the others were bathing, and then he wouldn't have to go into the water. He took up his pail and his shrimping-net and off he went along the sand, not looking back once, in case his mother should call to him.

And that was how he found the very queer pool among the rocks. He walked along for some way and came to some high rocks, covered with pretty green seaweed. There was nobody there at all. He was quite alone. He walked round one of the big rocks, and then he saw, set cosily in the midst of a ring of tall rocks, the loveliest pool he had ever seen. Seaweed hung down into it and waved about in the clear green water. The sand at the bottom was as yellow as the dandelions, and here and there in the water swam little glittering, brightly coloured creatures.

Mark stared at them. He couldn't think what they were. They were not like any fish he had ever seen, and they were too big for prawns or shrimps. They couldn't be crabs, and he knew that starfish couldn't swim like that. So what could they be?

"I'll put in my shrimping-net, and see if I can catch one," he said to himself, in great excitement. So he waded at the edge of the warm pool and pushed his net in front of him. He took it out quickly, and sure enough, he had caught one of the curious little glittering creatures.

How surprised he was to find he had caught a water-pixie! In his net, gasping and panting, lay a little fairy-like creature, with long, wet, golden hair, and a dress made of brightly coloured scales, like a fish's skin, that came down to her bare knees.

Mark almost dropped his net in surprise. Then afraid that the little thing would die out of water, just as a fish does, he filled his pail full of water and gently dropped the pixie into it. At once it began to swim about, and its hair floated out in the water like fine golden seaweed. It made funny little mewing noises as if it were frightened.

Mark sat down and looked at it in great astonishment. Should he take it back to show his Mummy and Daddy? It was really a very surprising thing.

Then he heard a very high little voice calling to him from the pool, and he saw one of the water-pixies climbing out on to the rock beside him. The little creature put its tiny hand on his bare arm, and spoke to him.

17

"Please, please, let my sister go! Don't take her away from us. She will die of fright if you do. Oh, be kind, little boy, and put her back. See how frightened she is!"

Mark looked into his pail. The little pixie there *was* very frightened. Mark felt very sorry for her. He knew how afraid he felt sometimes when he had to go into the sea and didn't want to – so he knew just how the water-pixie was feeling.

"All right!" he said to the little creature beside him. "I'll put your sister back. I don't want to frighten her."

He gently tipped the pail up and emptied the pixie back into the pool. At once there was a great cry of joy, and to Mark's surprise about a hundred of the tiny water-creatures suddenly climbed out of the water and clambered all over him, hugging him with their tiny wet arms.

"You're a good, kind boy!" they cried, in their high twittering voices. "Tell us what you would like and we'll do it for you."

"There isn't anything I'd like, thank you," said Mark. "I've got everything I want, and besides, I don't want you to give me anything just for being kind. I wouldn't have hurt one of you for anything."

"Come into the pool and play with us!" cried the pixie he had put back, and she dragged at him with her little hands.

"No, thank you," said Mark. "I'm not very fond of bathing in the water. I'm afraid of the sea, you know. I wish I wasn't."

"He's wished a wish!" cried all the pixies together.

"He's wished a wish! We'll make it come true! Come into the pool, Mark. Look, eat the little red end of that sea-weed near you, and you'll soon be as little as we are, so that we can play together."

18

Mark did as he was told – and no sooner had he eaten the red piece of seaweed than he felt himself slipping down and down off the rock, and then, splash! he was in the pool, which seemed suddenly to have grown as big as a lake – for Mark had grown as small as the pixies, and now no bigger than a small fish.

"Do you like it, Mark?" asked the pixies, swimming round him. Mark found himself swimming easily here and there, and he could breathe the air in the water just like a fish. It was wonderful, and very exciting!

"This is lovely!" he cried, and his voice was high and twittering like the pixies. "Oh, if only I could feel like this always, I would never mind bathing in the sea with my Mummy and Daddy."

"The tide is soon coming in," said one of the pixies. "Then we shall get some big waves to ride on. Will you like that, Mark?"

"No, I don't think so," said Mark. "I'm afraid of big waves."

"Oh, you just want to ride on one of the white horses of the sea," said a pixie, "and you'll never be afraid again."

"What's a white horse of the sea?" asked Mark, swimming about merrily.

"Oh, don't you know?" asked the pixie, swimming close behind him. "They gallop under the water on a rough day, and they just show their white manes above the surface of the sea. Haven't you seen them? They are so curly and white!"

"Oh, yes!" said Mark, surprised. "I've often seen what I thought were the white tops of the waves, but I didn't know they were really the manes of sea-horses."

"The tide is coming in!" cried the pixies, and Mark saw

a big wave sweep round the rock and splash into the pool with a flurry of foam. "Don't be afraid, Mark, we'll take care of you. Come on, we'll swim out of the pool now, into the sea. It has come right up to our pool!"

So out of the pool they went, and soon Mark found himself in the sea. He bumped into shrimps once or twice, and they darted off in fright. Once a pixie took him down to the sand bottom to show him a big starfish.

"Look at his mouth right in the middle of him," she said. "Isn't he a funny creature – just a mouth and five arms! And, oh, look! There's a jelly-fish floating along. Don't go too near, Mark, or it will hurt you. Those hairs hanging down will sting you if you touch them."

Mark saw a big umbrella-like jelly-fish floating along towards him and he quickly got out of its way. He went down to the sandy bottom again with the pixies and waited till the big jelly-fish had gone safely by.

Suddenly he felt something pinch his foot, and he gave a shout of pain. He looked down and saw that his foot was held in a pair of pincers.

"What is it?" he cried. "Oh, look, pixies, something has got hold of my foot."

"It's all right," said the pixies, laughing, "you're treading on a crab that has buried itself in the sand, that's all! It doesn't like being trodden on, so it's just telling you it's there!"

"Well, tell it to let go," said Mark. "I don't like being pinched!"

"Let go, crab!" commanded the pixies, "or we will dig you out of the sand and chase you into the deep waters, where you will get lost!"

The crab let go, and Mark took his foot away. The crab heaved itself out of the sand where it had been hiding and ran away sideways as fast as ever it could. It looked very comical and everybody laughed.

"Come on," said the pixies to Mark. "We want to go farther out to sea, where it is very deep."

Mark felt rather frightened, but the pixies took hold of his hands and swam along quickly with him. Suddenly, they dived down to the bottom again and Mark was pulled down with them. He was just in time to see two queer, pink things, waving above his head, very big and long.

"What were those?" he asked, frightened.

"Oh, those were the legs of somebody bathing," said the pixies. "It's best to get out of the way or we might get kicked. Hurry, Mark, because we still have a good way to go."

"Where are we going?" asked Mark, swimming along as fast as he could.

"To the stables of the sea horses," said the pixies. "We will all get a sea-horse to ride, and we will gallop to shore in a trice! It will be exciting, I can tell you!"

"But I don't think I want to," said Mark, frightened. "I can ride a donkey, but I've never ridden a horse. Suppose I fall off?"

"You can't fall off a sea-horse!" answered the pixies, in their twittering voices. "Be brave, just this once, Mark. After you've ridden a sea-horse under the water you will always love the sea and never be afraid of it again."

On they went, and on, and soon they met big fishes who opened their mouths wide as they swam. Mark was afraid of them at first, but he soon saw that they took no notice at all of the gay little pixies. One bold little fellow jumped on a cod's back and rode on him for quite a long way! All the others laughed loudly when the cod suddenly shot upwards and made the pixie fall off!

"Nearly there!" said the pixies beside Mark, and she pointed to a big white building at the bottom of the sea. It had wide double doors made entirely of sea-shells, and all around were planted waving seaweed trees.

"What place is this?" asked Mark.

"It's the stables of the sea-horses!" cried the pixies, joyfully. They swam down to the shell-doors and hammered on them with their small fists. At once the doors swung open and a merman looked out. He was a strange creature, with a long fish-tail instead of legs, and his hair was made of green seaweed. He had very bright eyes, and he wore a limpet shell for a hat.

"Hallo, hallo!" he cried. "So you're back again, are you! I suppose you want to ride on the sea-horses again! Well, they are all here, waiting for you! But mind you bring them back again once they reach the shore. Don't gallop them out on the sand, or they will run away on the beach and never come back again. Keep them well under the sea."

The pixies ran into the stables and took Mark with them. Then he saw the sea-horses. They were wonderful creatures, as white as snow with long curling manes and tails that waved about in the water. They had long slender legs and eyes as bright as diamonds, and they pawed the sand, eager for a gallop.

"Choose a gentle one for Mark!" said the pixies to the merman. "He's not used to sea-horses, and we don't want him to be thrown off."

Mark felt frightened again. "Perhaps I'd better not ride one," he said in a small voice.

"Pooh!" cried the pixie next to him. "Don't be silly, Mark! It's fine to ride a galloping sea-horse. You won't fall off if we choose a nice gentle one that doesn't go too fast. And remember, Mark, that once you have ridden a

22

sea-horse you will never, *never*, NEVER be afraid of the sea again!"

Well, Mark thought it would be lovely not to be frightened of the sea any more, so he climbed up on to the back of the big white horse that the merman chose for him. It had a broad, soft back, and it put its nose round to Mark and nuzzled his hand lovingly. It was a nice horse and Mark liked it. Its mane was very thick and curly, just like the tops of waves, and as white as snow. Its tail was curly too, and hung down nearly to the sand when it was not waving it about in the water.

The white horse cantered out of the stables and each one of them had a water-pixie on its broad back. The merman made them all stand in a straight row and then he lifted up a trumpet-like shell to his mouth and blew a loud blast.

At once all the horses shot off through the water like arrows. They rose up to the surface so that their white manes showed above the water, but no more. The pixies shouted to Mark to keep his horse's head down beneath the water.

"Only let his white mane show!" they cried. "If he puts his head out the wind will take his breath and he will choke."

Mark was full of joy and excitement. It was quite easy to keep on his horse's back, and he managed to pull his horse's head down so that only the white curly mane showed on the top of the sea. All the horses raced towards the shore, and the people lying on the sands sat up and said: "The sea is getting quite rough! All the waves have white crests!"

They didn't know it was really the white curly manes of the sea-horses that they saw!

Mark shouted to his horse to go on. He wanted to win the race! His horse darted forward and was soon in front of everyone else. What a shouting and calling there was!

Mark's winning, Mark's winning!" shouted the pixies. "He's nearly there! Be careful not to gallop your horse on to the shore, Mark, or he will run away!"

But, dear me, Mark couldn't stop his horse, and it suddenly ran right out of the sea and up the shore. It shook Mark off its back and then ran off like the wind, leaving the little boy lying out of breath on the sand.

"Oh, my goodness!" said Mark, sitting up. "I say, pixies, I'm so sorry, but my horse has run away!"

He heard the sound of an excited twittering of small voices and then he saw someone standing over him. It was his Daddy!

"Why, Mark, did that big wave knock you over?" said his Daddy. "I saw a great wave rush up the sand and when it had gone I saw you lying there. It must have knocked you over."

"Oh, no, Daddy, that wasn't a wave," said Mark. "That was a sea-horse you saw. I was riding it."

"You must have been asleep and dreaming," said his Daddy laughing, and he wouldn't believe anything that Mark told him about his sea adventures.

"I'll believe them if you're not afraid of the sea any more!" he said, with a laugh. "If you really *did* ride a sea-horse, Mark, you will never again be afraid of paddling or bathing, will you?"

"Of course not," said Mark at once. "I'm going to put my bathing-suit on and bathe now, this very minute, Daddy. Then you'll see I'm not afraid any more!"

And to his Daddy's great surprise, that is just exactly

The Tiny Water-creatures clambered all over him

what Mark did! He slipped into his bathing-suit and ran straight into the sea, although there were some big waves rolling in. He was not a bit afraid!

"Well, well," said Daddy and Mummy, in astonishment. "You *must* have had all those adventures, Mark! What a very strange thing! Do let's go and see if we can find that pixie-pool next time the tide is out."

They are going to try and find it tomorrow. I wonder if they will. Mark says if he does find it, he is going to show it to all the boys and girls that are afraid of the water – for then they can ride on sea-horses, too, and become as brave as he is!

Do you want to ride on a sea-horse? If you do, be sure to tell Mark when you meet him.

The Beautiful New Suit

Nobody liked Mister Cherry-Red very much. He was a good-looking gnome with blue eyes and a cheery-red mouth that didn't smile as much as it might. He was the vainest fellow in Wumple Village, and he liked nothing better than to be praised for his looks or his clothes.

One day the chief gnome of the village decided to give a large party. It was to be a very grand affair, and the Prince of the country would probably come, so everybody would have to get new clothes and be very smart indeed.

The invitations were sent out. Mister Cherry-Red had one, of course, and what a state of excitement he was in! Really, you should have seen him! He put the card on the

26

mantelpiece and walked up and down looking at it.

"Ho, so the Prince is coming, is he!" he thought. "Well, I shall get the grandest suit I've ever had – and the finest hat to match – and I shall ask to be presented to the Prince, and perhaps he will want me to go and stay with him. My, that will make the people of Wumple Village sit up and take notice of *me*. They haven't been too nice to me lately – jealous of my fine clothes, I suppose!"

But, you know, the people of Wumple were not jealous of Cherry-Red's clothes – no, not a bit. They hadn't been nice to him simply because he was getting too vain for anything. It was most tiresome to see him walking through the village all dressed up, looking for everyone to tell him how fine he was. No wonder the gnomes looked the other way!

Mister Cherry-Red went to Snips, his tailor, in the next town, and ordered a new suit and hat for the grand party.

"It shall be cherry-red, like my name," he said to the small dwarf who stood bowing before him. "I will have buttons down the front and down the back, too, and beautiful trousers with a black stripe down their cherry-redness! My, won't the Prince stare when he sees me! He will think I am a lord or prince, too!"

"You are better-looking than any prince, Mister Cherry-Red," said the dwarf, who was very pleased to hear that his customer wanted such a grand suit.

"Yes," said Cherry-Red, looking at himself in the glass. "I am rather good-looking, am I not? Ha, Snips, I'll be finer than the Prince when you have finished with me. Now, what about a hat? I'll have a very large one, I think, and it shall be cherry-red like the suit. You can cover the hat with some of the suit-cloth, Snips – and put a long, black feather in it, one that will almost sweep the ground.

And I'll have a black stick with a cherry-red handle. Ho, ho! Everyone will notice Mister Cherry-Red on the day of the party!"

"Very well, sir," said Snips. "It will be rather expensive, but I suppose you don't mind that?"

"Oh, yes I do," said Cherry-Red, hurriedly, for though he liked fine things, he was a mean fellow and hated to pay a lot for them. "Don't you charge me too much, now."

"Well, sir, look at this lovely cloth," said Snips, bringing out a roll of cherry-red cloth that was just the right colour. "This is the best I have. The suit will cost you twenty gold pieces."

"Far too much, far too much!" cried Cherry-Red, angrily. "What about that cloth over there? That is the right colour, and I am sure it will not be as expensive."

Snips took up the roll of cloth and shook his head. "It's the right colour," he said, "but I wouldn't like you to have a suit made of it, sir, really I wouldn't. It isn't a very good cloth. It might lose its colour – or shrink – or wear out very quickly."

"Now you are only just saying that because you want me to have that very expensive cloth you first showed me!" said Cherry-Red, in a fine temper. "You just make my suit of *this* cloth, and if you charge me a penny more than ten gold pieces I'll never come to you again!"

"Very good, sir," said Snips, and he bowed Mister Cherry-Red out of the shop. He set to work on the suit and a very good job he made of it, too. It was just exactly right for Cherry-Red, and fitted him like a glove. The buttons at the front and back shone and twinkled as he walked, and the hat sat on his curly head with its long black feather sweeping right down to the ground. He did look grand! He stood in front of the glass and looked at himself with pleasure. He was surely the best-looking and the finest-dressed gnome in the whole of the kingdom.

"I shall send a note to the chief gnome and tell him that I expect him to present me to the Prince," said Cherry-Red to himself. He did so – and was most delighted when the chief sent to say that he would be pleased to present him.

Cherry-Red put away his new suit, hat, and stick very carefully until the great day came. He looked anxiously out of the window on the morning of the day, and was disappointed to see large clouds in the sky.

"I do hope it won't rain," he thought. "It would quite spoil everything if I had to take an umbrella. I do want to take my new stick. An umbrella would look so foolish with that cherry-red suit."

At three o'clock Mister Cherry-Red began to dress. On went his new suit, with the twinkling buttons. His trousers came nicely down to his feet and fitted him tightly, except at the ankles where they swung out like a sailor's trousers. He put on his hat and the feather waved this way and that. He took up his stick – and he was ready.

He went to the front door. Going by were other gnomes of the village, on their way to the party. Mister Cherry-Red looked at them. How plain and dowdy they seemed! What was the matter with everyone?

Then he saw that most of the gnomes wore mackintoshes, or else they carried umbrellas, for the large, black clouds were still sailing across the sky. He frowned.

"I am sure it won't rain," he said to himself. "How could it rain when I have such a grand new suit? I couldn't bear to wear a mackintosh. I should hate to take an umbrella. I shan't take either. I shall arrive at the party just as I am, in all the grandness of my new suit and swinging my fine stick in my hand!"

He set off. He meant to go through the woods where the elves lived, so that they might peep out of their homes and admire him, the great Mister Cherry-Red. It would be a rare treat for them to see him go by!

He walked between the trees, and the elves came out to look at him. Certainly he was a very grand sight indeed. One little elf cried out. "Oh, is he the Prince?"

That made Mister Cherry-Red feel very delighted. He stalked along, his head in the air, swinging his stick to and fro.

And then a dreadful thing happened.

It poured with rain! An enormous cloud came overhead, and down came the rain in torrents! It soaked poor Mister Cherry-Red from head to foot in two minutes, for he had no umbrella. He stood and gasped in dismay. Whatever was he to do?

A small elf looked out from a hollow tree and smiled to see Cherry-Red gasping in the rain like a fish out of water.

"The sun will be out in a moment," he said, pointing to the sky. "Don't worry. It is very hot, and will soon dry your things again."

Mister Cherry-Red looked up at the sky. The cloud was going. The rain stopped. The sun shone out, very hot indeed. He looked down at his drenched clothes.

"I shall take them off and hang them on a bush to dry," he thought sadly. "I shall be late for the party, but never mind. The others will stare at me all the more when I come in, and think how grand I am."

He took off his trousers and his coat. They were so wet that he had to squeeze them to get out some of the rain. He took off his hat, and shook it. The feather looked very sorry for itself now. He hung the hat on a branch.

The elves came round him and giggled. Poor Mister Cherry-Red sat on the grass in his long vest, and looked very funny. It was a blue vest, and had two or three holes in, for although Mister Cherry-Red liked to be very grand in his suits, he wasn't very careful about darning underneath. He sat there and waited patiently for his suit to dry.

The sun shone and shone. It was certainly very hot indeed. Cherry-Red felt hot even in his vest. He got up and felt his suit – and then he looked at it in dismay. The lovely red colour had run, and the suit was pink here and there instead of red! Oh, dear, oh, dear! How dreadful!

"Well, perhaps people will think it is meant to be pink and red," thought Mister Cherry-Red, looking at his watch. "Anyway, the buttons are all right – and the black feather in the hat has dried, and is as fine as ever. And my stick looks lovely. I'll put my things on now – it is getting late and I really must go."

He took his trousers from the branch where they hung, and began to put them on – but, my goodness me, what do you suppose? They had shrunk with the rain, and Cherry-Red could hardly get into them! They were dreadfully tight, and the buttons of the trousers were up to his knees! The coat was just the same – the cuffs were up to the elbows, and he couldn't button up the front because the edges wouldn't meet!

Mister Cherry-Red could have wept with despair. He dragged the coat together – and there came a tearing noise. It had split along the shoulders! He certainly couldn't wear it now! He put on his hat. That was much too small, though the feather still swept down to the ground.

"I can't go to the party!" wept Mister Cherry-Red. "I can't go to the party. My trousers are too small. My coat is split. I can't go in a vest and a hat. I must go home and put on my old suit. Boo, hoo, hoo!"

"Ho, ho, ho!" chuckled all the elves, most amused to see the grand gnome walking off in a vest and hat. Cherry-Red looked at them angrily. He rolled up his trousers and his coat and threw them at the giggling elves. One of them picked them up and put them on, dancing about in them gleefully.

Horrid little creatures!" thought the gnome, marching off. "I wish I'd never walked through the woods to show myself off to them now."

He came to the edge of the woods and walked down the lane that led to his cottage. He turned the corner, and, to his great horror, he saw a carriage and pair outside his house! The chief gnome, wondering why Cherry-red had not come to his party, had taken the Prince on a tour round his pretty little village, and had stopped at the gnome's house to see if anything was wrong with him.

"Oh, there he is!" cried the chief, pointing to Cherry-Red coming down the lane. "Hi, Cherry-Red! Why didn't you come to the party? Here is the Prince. Come and meet him."

Poor, poor Mister Cherry-Red! Whatever could he do? There he stood in his torn blue vest and black hat, too small for him, stammering and gulping.

"Why does he walk about in a vest?" asked the Prince, in surprise. He really thought Cherry-Red must be mad.

"I g-g-g-got c-c-caught in the r-r-ain!" said poor Cherry-Red. "My suit shrank, and I th-th-threw it away. Boo, hoo, hoo!"

"Oh, dear, Cherry-Red, how dreadful for you!" said

32

Mister Cherry-Red could have wept with despair

the chief gnome, trying not to laugh. "Excuse me smiling, but really, you do look very funny."

"Ho, ho, ho!" roared all the gnomes around.

"Boo, hoo, hoo!" cried Cherry-Red, and he ran up his garden-path and into his cottage. He slammed the door, and sat down on a chair. He put his face into his hands and wept and wept till his tears made a puddle on the floor.

"It's my own fault!" he sobbed. "I wanted to be grand – and I was mean and wouldn't pay enough for a good suit – and I wanted to show off to the elves – and I hadn't got my mackintosh or umbrella, because I wanted to look fine. I am a very foolish gnome – and I didn't like walking home in my vest – and I can't go to the party – and whatever will the Prince say to me? Oh, oh, I am *so* unhappy! I will never be vain again."

What a joke they had at the party, everyone talking about Mister Cherry-Red walking home in his vest! How they laughed! How they chuckled!

"It will do him good to look foolish," said the gnomes. "He won't show off quite so much in future. If he does we know what to say to him."

They did – for whenever Mister Cherry-Red came out in any new clothes, and looked all conceited, one of the gnomes would slip up to him and say: "Good-day, Cherry-Red – have you mended the holes in your vest? You never know when you might have to walk home in it, you know!"

Then the gnome would go as red as his name, and hang his head. Poor old Cherry-Red!

What Happened To Eppie

Eppie was a little shepherd boy. He looked after sheep on the mountain-side, and his uncle watched them with him. They had two dogs, swift runners, who could outrun any wolf and hunt it down.

There were many, many sheep, spread all over the mountain-side. Sometimes Eppie had to go up and down, seeking for two or three that had strayed, or had hurt themselves. A dog went with him then for company. Eppie liked the spring and the summer, for then the days were golden and the nights were warm. But when the winter came he shivered and wished that he could be a little town boy, safe in a warm house at night, instead of taking turns with his uncle at watching the sheep.

The big, grey wolves were hungry in the winter-time, and came slinking out of their mountain lairs to hunt for food. Sometimes they came to the flock of sheep and stole a lamb. Eppie had to watch for the creeping form against the side of the hill, outlined by the moonlight. Then he would give the alarm, and the dogs would wake and race after the wolf.

One winter Eppie was lazy and discontented. He grumbled all day long and his uncle grew vexed with him.

"You are a young lad, and must learn to work," said his uncle sharply. "Enough of this grumbling. Eppie, or I will beat you!"

"This is no life for a boy," sulked Eppie. "I hate the silly grey sheep. I hate the stupid, skipping lambs."

"You are a bad boy to say such things," said his uncle, and beat him. "The sheep give us warm clothes and good meat, and as for the little lambs, they are pretty creatures and sweet to watch in the spring-time. You cannot help loving such innocent things. Let me hear no more of your stupidity, Eppie, or you will have a beating each day."

Eppie said no more, for he was afraid of his tall, strong uncle, with his brown weather-beaten face. The shepherd was a fine man, tender with the little lambs and good to the sheep when they were hurt or needed his help. He could not understand why Eppie did not love the flock as he did.

That night Eppie had to watch the sheep. It was cold, and the moon shone pale in the sky. Eppie shivered and pulled his rug round him. The two dogs lay at his feet, tired out with a long run that afternoon, rounding up stray sheep. They lay with their noses to their feet, dreaming of rabbits and wolves.

Eppie's uncle was in a hut a good way up the mountain. Round it were sheltering hurdles to keep in the sheep that had little new-born lambs. The shepherd was going to be up all night, tending them, and he had warned Eppie to keep a good watch that night.

"The big grey wolf is about," he said. "He took a sheep from over the hills, so I heard, not three days ago. Watch well, Eppie."

Eppie did not answer. He turned away, sulking. He was tired, and wanted to sleep. He felt sure that his uncle had made up the tale about the wolf, in order to frighten him and make him alert.

"There's no wolf about!" he thought. "I don't believe my uncle's tale."

He sat in the shelter of a rock, wrapped in a thick blanket. The stars were pale in the moonlight. He could see clearly the valley, below, with black shadows here and there, cast by bushes and trees. Nothing moved but the grey sheep, and even they were very still that night. There were some tiny lambs here and there with their mothers, and they lifted their heads, maa-ing now and again.

Eppie felt sleepy. He knew he should get up and walk about to keep himself awake. But he was sulky and bad tempered, and would not move. His eyes kept shutting.

"What does it matter if I sleep?" he thought. "No wolf will come! And if one does come, what will happen? A few lambs will be frightened, and maybe one carried off. Shepherds expect that now and again. What do I care for the silly lambs? I shall sleep!"

He closed his eyes, and soon, like the two dogs, he was fast asleep and dreaming. Two hours passed. No wolf came – but someone else did! The boy's uncle stole down the hill like a black shadow, come to tell Eppie to go to the hut and take his rest whilst he watched instead. When he found Eppie fast asleep he was very angry. He saw the boy's sulky face, and then was sad, too. Eppie had to be a shepherd, and until he cared for the flock, and loved the lambs, he would not be happy. The shepherd looked down at the sleeping boy, and then sat quietly down by him. He began to murmur a tale into the boy's ear – and Eppie dreamed the tale!

In his dream he was a lamb, small and long-legged, with a wriggling tail. He was on the mountain-side in the warm sunshine, skipping all about with joy. His small brother was with him, and together they bounded here and there, rushing to their big warm mother when she baa-ed at them. Life was good. Everything was warm, and the little lamb was full of delight.

But when the night came it was different. The big golden

37

ball in the sky went away, and the darkness came. The moon rose, but it was not full and gave only a pale light to the world. Everything looked different. The air was cold and the tiny lamb shivered. He cuddled close to his mother and she licked him and his little brother tenderly.

The lamb had heard of the wolf, but it was only at night that he was afraid of it.

"What is the wolf?" he asked his mother.

"It is a great grey shape in the night-time," answered his mother. "It has red, gleaming eyes and fearful gleaming teeth. It comes like a shadow, and eats little lambs like you. So keep close to me."

The lamb cuddled even closer, and maa-ed in fright.

"Do not be afraid," said the mother sheep, comfortingly. "We have a good shepherd to watch over us, and a boy, too. There are two dogs, besides. See, the boy is watching us now, through the night, and if the wolf should come, he will give the alarm and wake the dogs. Then they will chase the wolf away and no harm will be done!"

After that the mother sheep fell asleep, and the lamb and his brother closed their eyes and slept, too – but in a short while the little lamb awakened with a start, full of fear. He stared round in the night. The moon was behind a cloud and the mountain-side was in darkness. What had wakened him?

A feeling of dreadful fear came over the little creature. Something terrible was near him. What was it? And then he saw two red, gleaming eyes in the darkness! It was the wolf, the wolf! It was looking at him. It was coming to take him away!

Where was the shepherd boy? Could he not see the wolf? Would he not send the dogs chasing after him down the hill-side? Oh, shepherd boy, wake up, wake up! The two eyes came nearer still, and the little lamb dared not move. He could hear the wolf sniffing, and then he felt the animal's hot breath over him.

"Maa-aa!" he called, pressing against his mother. She woke and smelt the wolf at once. In terror she scrambled to her feet and bounded away, calling loudly to her two lambs. One ran with her – but the other, who had waked to see the wolf near, could not get away. The wolf bared his teeth and snatched at him.

"Maa-aa!" bleated the lamb piteously. Where, oh where was the shepherd boy? Surely he could not be asleep? Where were the two swift-running dogs?

The wolf picked up the shivering lamb in his sharp teeth and made off with him. "Maa-aa, maa-aa!" bleated the lamb in terror. Then the whole flock was aroused and bunched together quickly, baa-ing loudly. The two dogs awoke, rushed here and there, trying to get the trail of the wolf. They quickly found it and were after him in a trice.

The little lamb heard the dogs barking. The wolf gripped him even more tightly in his teeth and the lamb bleated in pain. Suddenly the two dogs appeared, one on each side of the wolf, and the wolf dropped the lamb, bared its teeth and faced the dogs. The lamb lay still, terrified. He was not badly hurt, but so full of fear that he could not even move his head.

The dogs leaped on the wolf, and it backed away snarling. The lamb heard the fighting getting farther and farther away, and then suddenly saw a swinging light. Was it another wolf? He maa-ed in terror – but it was the lantern of the shepherd. Then the tiny lamb felt himself gathered up in the arms of someone who loved him and he was full of peace and happiness. He was safe.

The little shepherd boy, whose dream this was, suddenly felt himself picked up in someone's strong arms. He

39

was the little lamb and the shepherd boy, too. How strange! He awoke and opened his eyes. Now he was only a shepherd boy, out on the mountain-side. He was no longer a wolf-hunted lamb. He was in the arms of his uncle, the shepherd who was carrying him up the mountain-side to the hut.

"Uncle, Uncle, put me down; there is a wolf among the sheep!" he cried, struggling, half remembering his strange dream. "Oh, quick, the little lambs will be so frightened. They may be caught in the teeth of that big grey wolf. Oh, uncle, let me go and see if the sheep are all right. Let me take the dogs!"

"There is no wolf tonight," said his uncle. "You are tired with your long day with the dogs, Eppie. I came to take your place, and found you sleeping, so I am carrying you to the hut. It seemed a shame to wake you."

"Uncle, I had such a strange dream," said Eppie, remembering how he had seemed to be a little lamb. "Do you know how frightened a lamb can be, Uncle? I dreamed I was caught by a wolf. It was terrible. I shall never sleep again when it is my turn to watch! The sheep trust us, Uncle, don't they?"

"Yes," said his uncle. "I think you will be a good shepherd boy now, won't you, Eppie?"

"Yes, always," said Eppie, and he meant it. "It is a grand thing to be a shepherd, Uncle. One day I shall be the best shepherd in the kingdom, and have the biggest flocks in the world!"

The Artful Pixie

Once upon a time the people of Heyho Land were in a very bad way, because two powerful people lived there – a Wumple Witch and a Whistling Wizard. The Witch lived down in the plains, and frightened all the people there, and the Wizard lived up in the hills, and scared the shepherds a dozen times a week.

So you see, it wasn't a bit of good moving to get away from the Witch because then the people lived too near the Wizard; or if they moved away from the Wizard, they came across the Witch. It was all most upsetting.

If only the Wumple Witch and the Whistling Wizard had kept to their own work, and left the people of Heyho alone, it would have been all right. But they didn't leave them alone. They were always borrowing their black cats to help them to make spells, or stealing their broom-sticks to fly about on, or even making the people themselves work for them.

One day the Wumple Witch made a mistake in one of her spells, which was to make a saucepan that would boil without a fire beneath it; and because of the mistake every single saucepan in the land jumped off the stove and ran off to goodness knows where. Anyhow, they were never seen again, and that made the people of Heyho very angry.

Then the very next week the Wizard played a trick on everyone, just for fun. He whistled for the wind, and whispered something in his ear – and in a trice the wind went off and flicked away everybody's hat! It brought them all to the Wizard and laid them down in a neat row at his feet.

The people didn't dare to complain, but they were most annoyed. It meant that everyone had to go and buy a new hat, and as the Whistling Wizard owned the only hat shop in the town, he made quite a lot of money out of his trick.

"What can we do to get rid of the Wumple Witch and the Whistling Wizard?" groaned the people, when they met one another in the street. "Let's have a secret meeting about it."

So they did – but not even the wisest of them could think of a really safe way to get rid of them. Everyone was too much afraid. And then a small pixie, called Kiki, got up and spoke.

"I believe I have an idea," he said, in his high, little voice. "*We* can't get rid of the Witch and the Wizard – but why not let them get rid of each other?"

"It *sounds* very clever," said Bron, the head brownie. "But how can it be done? You are full of ideas, Kiki, but they are not much good when we try to carry them out!"

"All right!" said Kiki, offended. "I'll do the idea myself! I won't tell you anything about it! But what will you give me if I manage to get rid of the Wumple Witch and the Whistling Wizard? Tell me that!"

Bron, the brownie, didn't believe that the sharp-eyed little pixie would do anything very clever, so he laughed and said: "Oh, you shall be King of Heyho, if you *do* manage to get rid of those two nuisances – but you won't!"

Kiki's eyes grew very bright. He skipped out of the meeting-hall and went to his tiny cottage. It was very bare and shabby, for Kiki was poor. But soon he would be rich!

He would be King of Heyho! He would have a carriage and pair! Oho! wouldn't everyone stare at him!

He sat down on a three-legged stool and thought hard. Then he took up his bag of tools, and put on his leather apron and set off to the castle in the plain where lived the powerful Wumple Witch. Kiki was a carpenter by trade, and he often went round the countryside offering to mend things for people – a broken chair, a shelf, and things like that.

Now he went to the Wumple Witch. He knocked boldly on the door of the castle, and the big black cat, who was the chief servant of the Witch, opened the door to him.

"I'm Kiki the carpenter," said the pixie. "Any jobs want doing, sir? I can mend anything that's made of wood!"

The black cat was so delighted at being called "sir", that he bade Kiki come in. "Yes," he said, "there's a-many jobs want doing in this place. It's hard to get a carpenter in, for they're all afraid of the Witch, and *she* is too busy to bother about mending things that break!"

Kiki went in and set to work on a dozen broken things. He put a new leg on a table; he put up two shelves in the kitchen; the made a new door for a cupboard. He worked so quickly and so well that the black cat spoke to the Wumple Witch about him.

"Your Highness," said the cat to the Witch, "there's a clever little fellow here, mending things in the kitchen. Would you like him to mend your magic wand for you – the one that broke in half when you hit me with it? And what about your biggest broomstick? That could do with mending, too, I think, because it's getting old and soon won't bear us both when we go flying on it at night."

"All right, bring him in, and I'll tell him what I want done," said the Witch. This was just what Kiki wanted.

He skipped into the Witch's strange workroom, which was full of green smoke, and bowed to her.

"I want you to mend that and that," said the Witch, pointing to the wand and the broomstick.

"I'm sorry," said Kiki. I haven't time to stop. I've got to go and mend for someone else tomorrow."

"Oh!" said the Witch, frowning in a most terrifying manner. "And who is more important than I am, I should like to know?"

"The Whistling Wizard, up in the hills," said Kiki, at once. "He's much cleverer than you are. He can do heaps of things you can't do. Oh, he's a wonderful fellow, and everyone thinks so!"

The Wumple Witch looked as black as thunder.

"Well, you tell the Whistling Wizard *this*!" she said angrily. "You tell him that if he likes I'll meet him somewhere and show him how much cleverer I am than *he* is! Ho, ho! *I'll* show him a few things! And when I've shown him a little of what I can do, I'll send him whistling away to the moon!"

"But could you really do that?" asked Kiki, pretending to be most surprised. "I don't believe you!"

"Oh, don't you?" said the Witch. "Well, wait and see, that's all! Now go to the Wizard—and just tell him my message!"

Kiki went. He rode on a rabbit all the way to the hills, and the next morning he knocked on the Whistling Wizard's castle door. A grey goose opened it, the Wizard's latest servant. When she heard that Kiki could mend anything made of wood she bade him come in.

Soon he was busy mending chairs and cupboards. The Wizard passed him by one day and watched him.

"It's a pity you weren't here last week," he said. "I had

44

a magic candlestick that wanted mending, and you could have done it well."

"I couldn't have come last week," said Kiki, going on with his work. "I was working for somebody very important."

"Oh, indeed!" said the Wizard snappily. "And who is more important than I am, I should like to know?"

"Why, the Wumple Witch of course!" said Kiki. "She's very clever and very powerful – much more powerful than *you* are, Whistling Wizard!"

"What nonsense!" said the Wizard angrily. "Why, I could beat her at anything she liked to mention!"

"Oh, no, you couldn't!" said Kiki, hammering a nail into a chair-leg. "Oh, no! The Wumple Witch doesn't think much of *you*! She sent you a message to say she'll meet you any time you like, and show you what a stupid fellow you are compared with her! And what's more, she'll send you whistling away to the moon when she's finished with you!"

The Wizard was so tremendously astonished that for two whole minutes he really couldn't say a word. He just stood there, swallowing and gulping with rage. Kiki looked at him.

"Don't be frightened," he said, pretending that he thought the Wizard was terrified. "I'll see she doesn't really hurt you! I don't expect she'll send you whistling to the moon unless you annoy her."

Well! The Wizard simply exploded with rage! You should have seen him! He went red in the face, and then purple, and then black! Kiki felt rather frightened but he didn't show it. He just went on hammering.

"You could go and tell the Wumple Witch I'll meet her in the Cowslip Meadow at twelve o'clock on Tuesday morning," he shouted. "And I'll show her a few things! Yes, I will! I'll send her down to the middle of the earth before I've done with her!"

Kiki gathered up his tools and ran off. He was overjoyed because his plan seemed to be acting so well. By the next morning he was knocking at the Wumple Witch's door, and the black cat let him in, quite pleased to see him.

"I've a message for the Wumple Witch," said Kiki, and he went to see her.

"Madam," he said. "I come from the Whistling Wizard. He laughs to think that you believe yourself to be more powerful than he is! He will meet you at twelve o'clock on Tuesday morning in Cowslip Meadow, and there he will show you how clever he is and how foolish *you* are! And to end with he'll send you off to the middle of the earth!"

The Wumple Witch shook so much with anger that her hat fell off. She picked it up and put it on again.

"I'll be there!" she said. "I'll be there!"

And she *was* there, exactly as the clock struck twelve on Tuesday morning. The Whistling Wizard was there too – and so was the grey goose, his servant. The Witch's black cat was there as well, making up his mind to eat the goose if he had a chance. And all the people of Heyho Land were there – but not too near, for sparks flew and flames shot up when witches and wizards quarrelled!

Well, the wonderful things they did! You should have seen them! The Wizard made a plum tree grow, and it grew so high that it touched the sky. The plums on it were as big as melons. Then he waved his stick and the plums changed to gold! It was marvellous.

The Witch said that was a silly trick, one she had learnt when she was three years old. She made a tall tower grow

46

out of the ground, and suddenly it arched over and changed into a fierce dragon which was just going to eat the Wizard's grey goose when the Witch laughed and made it disappear in smoke.

"Pooh!" said the Wizard. "A simple trick! Can you do nothing better than that?"

Ah, then they really go going! They changed themselves into lions and ogres, they made the thunder sound in the sky, and they caught the lightning and lighted candles with it. They cut pieces out of the clouds and made themselves purple and grey cloaks. And all the time they were watching for a chance to throw a spell on each other, for they were fiercely jealous of one another's power.

The watching people were frightened to see such magic. They wished they hadn't come. Only Kiki was delighted, for he felt sure that it would all end right.

Suddenly there was a pause in the magic. Neither Witch nor Wizard could think of anything more to do for the moment – and in that minute they weaved spells upon each other! The Wizard whispering a powerful fly-away spell to send the Witch to the middle of the earth – and the Witch murmured a marvellous fly-away spell to send the Wizard up to the moon!

They each guessed what the other was doing – but it was too late! Before the Wizard could stop himself he found that he was racing up through the air, off to the moon. And before the Witch could stop *herself*, she was sinking down, down, down to the very middle of the earth.

They were gone! Yes, they were gone! The Whistling Wizard was only a speck in the sky, and soon he had disappeared altogether. The ground closed over the Wumple Witch, and there was no sign of her either.

The watching people were frightened to see such Magic.

"They've gone, they've gone, they've gone!" cried all the people in excitement, and they clapped their hands for joy.

"Yes, and they won't come back!" said Kiki, feeling very grand. "I did it! I planned it all!"

"How?" cried everyone. "How?"

Then Kiki told them everything: and how they praised him and patted him on the back!

"You deserve to be our king!" they cried. "You do really! Come along and we'll crown you this very day.

So they crowned him king, and he had a carriage and pair, a palace, and as much as he liked to eat, which pleased him very much. He made a very good king, and was always fair and just.

As for the Whistling Wizard and the Wumple Witch, they were prisoners for ever. Some say that the Man in the Moon is no other than the Wizard – and others say that when there is an earthquake, it's just the Wumple Witch twisting and turning in the middle of the earth, trying her hardest to get free. But I really don't know about that.

The Clever White Kitten

Elsie was soon to have a birthday, and she felt most excited about it. She wondered if anyone would give her a pet for her birthday. She was very fond of animals and would love one for her very own.

"If I had a puppy or a little kitten, how lovely it would be!" she said to herself. "Or even a canary – but that would mean buying a cage, too, and that would be a lot of money. I should have to get a big cage too, because I wouldn't like to keep a canary in a tiny cage. Oh, dear, if only someone would buy me a pet!"

Elsie's mother had been thinking what to buy for Elsie, and she made up her mind to get her a nice work-basket, with a pair of scissors, a thimble, and reels of cotton in it. She thought Elsie would be so pleased to have one.

"What shall *I* buy for Elsie?" said the little girl's Daddy. "I wonder if she'd like a pet?"

"Oh, I don't think so," said Elsie's mother. "She has never said she wanted a pet."

That was quite true. Elsie had never said how much she would love an animal of her own. She had just hoped someone would buy her one. But they never seemed to think of a present like that!

Elsie's Daddy couldn't think of anything else to buy her, so he thought he would just give her ten shillings to spend on herself. Elsie's Mummy took the little girl with her to choose a nice work-basket at the shop, the day before her birthday.

The shop sold all sorts of baskets and leather goods. Elsie looked round. There were dog-baskets and cat-baskets, work-baskets, and shopping-baskets, purses and suit-cases, dog leads and collars. It was quite an exciting shop.

"I want a nice big work-basket for my little girl's birthday," said Elsie's mother. The shop-woman took some down. They were lovely, especially one, which was large and round, fitted inside with green silk on which lay a pair of shining scissors, a silver thimble, and four reels of cotton. Elsie liked it very much.

"I'll have that one," said her mother. "Will you send it round tonight, please? Thank you. And now I want to see purses for myself. Elsie, you can have a look round the shop whilst I choose them."

So Elsie wandered round the shop, looking at everything – and when she suddenly saw the little white kitten!

It was lying fast asleep in a round dog-basket, which was much too large for it! Elsie stroked it gently and it woke up at once. It stretched itself and yawned, and then rubbed its beautiful white head against the little girl's hand, purring loudly.

"Oh, you lovely, soft little thing!" said Elsie, cuddling the kitten against her. "I wish you were mine! What fun we would have together! I would give you a little basket of your own, and you should have bread and milk for your breakfast every morning. I would buy you a blue ribbon for your soft, white neck, and we would have the loveliest games!"

The kitten purred more loudly than ever. It liked Elsie very much. It cuddled down against her and patted her with one little white paw.

Another shop-girl came up and spoke to Elsie.

"The kitten is for sale," she said. "Would you like to buy it?"

"How much is it?" asked Elsie, remembering that she had tenpence in her money-box.

"Ten shillings," said the shop-girl. "It is a very good kitten. Mrs. Brown, the shopkeeper always gets ten shillings for the white kittens her cat has."

"I've only got tenpence," said Elsie sadly. "Oh, I wish Mummy had bought this kitten instead of the work-box."

She ran up to her mother and pulled her arm. "Mummy," she said, "I suppose I couldn't have something else instead of the work-basket, could I? I've just seen something much nicer."

"No, Elsie," said her mother. "You can't change your mind like that. You know you want a work-basket, don't you?"

"Yes, I do," said Elsie, "but Mummy, this is a dear little . . ."

"It doesn't matter *what* it is," said her mother, impatiently. "You have chosen your basket, and I am sure you will like it better than anything else. Besides, the shopwoman has made out the bill, and I have paid it. It is too late to change your mind now."

Elsie was sorry. She had so badly wanted that kitten. Her eyes filled with tears, and she ran back to the corner where the little kitten was jumping up at a fly.

It leapt into her arms as she came near it, quite certain that this nice little girl was going to buy it and take it home. It wanted to live with Elsie. It was quite sure it would be happy with the kind little girl. It was certain that she was going to take it home with her that very minute.

But Elsie stroked it and said no, she couldn't have it. "I'm having a work-basket instead," she told the kitten.

"That big round one there, on the counter. It is being sent round to my home tonight, so that I shall have it for my birthday in the morning. But, oh, kitten, I would so much rather have *you*!"

The kitten mewed and licked the back of Elsie's hand. It really was the dearest little kitten! It listened to all that Elsie said, and seemed to understand it.

"Good-bye," said Elsie, seeing her mother beckoning to her. "I wish you were mine!"

She went out of the shop with her mother, and the kitten was left alone, licking its fine white fur. It was thinking hard, for it was a very clever little kitten, especially when it wanted its own way. How could it go to that nice little girl? It wanted to live with her.

Then an idea came into its clever little mind. It would creep into the big round basket that was to be sent to Elsie that night, and then it would go to the little girl – and when she opened the basket in the morning she would see the little white kitten there!

"She is sure to keep me if I go to her," thought the kitten. It waited until the shop-woman had gone to her tea that afternoon, and then it ran to the work-basket which stood ready to be packed up. In a trice the kitten had lifted off the lid and had crept inside. There was just room for it to lie down. The lid dropped down on top of it – and there it was, curled up inside the basket.

It didn't make a sound. It soon fell fast asleep, and didn't even wake up when the shop-woman came to wrap the basket up in brown paper, ready for it to be taken to Elsie's home.

"Dear me! I didn't know this basket was so heavy!" said the shop-woman in surprise, but she didn't think of lifting up the lid to look inside! She gave the parcel to the

53

shop-girl to take to Elsie's house, and the girl carried it safely there, and gave it to the maid who opened the door.

That night Elsie's mother unwrapped the basket and set it on Elsie's chair, ready for the little girl to find when she came downstairs on her birthday morning. Her Daddy put a little envelope on top of it with some money in. That was *his* birthday present to her. Next to the basket was a doll from her aunt, and a book from her Granny. There was a pincushion from the cook, and a bottle of sweets from Jane the housemaid. So you see there were quite a lot of things waiting for Elsie!

Inside the work-basket was the kitten, too, waiting for Elsie. But nobody knew about that! When everyone had gone to sleep that night the kitten awoke. It lifted up the basket lid and crept out on to the chair. It wandered all round the house by itself, and smelt lots of mice.

"Ho!" said the kitten to itself. "Mice! I shall have a fine time here! I shall catch all the mice there are!"

Soon the kitten crept back into the basket again and fell asleep until morning. The housemaid came in and dusted the room. The kitten lay quiet. The cook came in and brought the scuttle full of coal. The kitten didn't move a whisker! Daddy came in and took up the paper. The kitten hardly breathed! Mummy came in and arranged the breakfast things just so. The kitten nearly burst with excitement, for it knew that Elsie would soon be there!

Then there was the sound of someone singing happily, and into the room came Elsie, singing: "It's my birthday, my birthday, my birthday!"

"Many happy returns of the day, little birthday girl!" cried Daddy and Mummy together, and they kissed her. "Come and look at all your lovely presents."

Elsie ran to her chair and looked at her presents. How

pleased she was with them! The doll was lovely, the book was fine, the sweets were just what she wanted, the pin-cushion was just right for her dressing-table, and the ten-shilling note from her Daddy was simply lovely!

"And thank you, Mummy darling, for the lovely, lovely work-basket!" she cried – and she opened the lid! There, curled up inside was the little white kitten, purring loudly its eyes blinking up at Elsie.

"Oooooh!" screamed the little girl in the greatest sur-prise and delight. "Ooh! Mummy! You darling, Mummy! What a surprise! Oh, you couldn't have given me anything I liked better! Oh, Mummy, I *shall* love this dear, little, white kitten!"

She lifted it out of the basket and hugged it. Mummy and Daddy stared in the greatest astonishment. They knew nothing about the kitten at all. How had it got there?

"A kitten!" cried Mummy. "Why, how did it get into the basket, Elsie? Where did it come from? I don't know anything about it."

"But, Mummy, it's the one from the basket shop," said Elsie. "Didn't you buy it for me and put it in here for a lovely birthday surprise?"

"No, I didn't, dear," said Mummy. "You will have to take it back to the shop, I'm afraid. They will wonder what has become of it."

"Then it isn't mine, after all?" asked Elsie, terribly disappointed. "Oh, Mummy, I did so think it was for me. Oh, Mummy, I do want it."

"But, darling, you can't possibly have it," said Mummy. "It isn't ours."

Elsie sat down to breakfast, but her birthday was spoilt. She did so want the kitten. Now she had got to take it back to the shop. The kitten must have wanted to belong to her,

There, curled up inside was the little white kitten

or it would never have hidden itself in the basket. What a horrid disappointment.

Tears fell into her corn-flakes and tears fell into her milk. Mummy saw them and was sorry.

"Don't cry, dear," she said. "It's your birthday, you know, and nobody must cry on birthdays. The postman hasn't been yet, and he may bring you some more parcels, so cheer up."

But even when the postman brought five birthday cards and three more parcels for Elsie, she didn't cheer up. She wanted that kitten. She gave it some milk and it drank it all up. Then it flew round the room like a mad thing after a bumble-bee. Then it curled up on Elsie's lap and fell asleep.

"You had better get your hat and coat on, and Daddy and I will go with you to take the kitten back to the shop," said Mummy. So Elsie sadly put on her coat and hat, and Mummy put the kitten gently into a box with holes in it. Then Daddy carried it carefully, and Mummy took Elsie's hand, and they all set off to the shop.

Mummy was sorry when she saw Elsie's sad face. "You are a silly child," she said. "Why didn't you tell me that you wanted a kitten for your birthday? Daddy would have given you one, or a puppy, if you really wanted one."

"But Mummy, I did ask you yesterday if I could change the work-basket for the kitten," said Elsie. "But you said it was too late to change my mind."

"Well, darling, I don't expect the shop would have let you have their kitten," said Mummy. "I'm sure the shop-woman must be very fond of it, and wouldn't want to part with it."

"But you don't *understand*, Mummy!" cried Elsie. "The kitten was for sale, just like all the baskets and things. The shop-girl said Mrs. Brown always sold the white kittens, and she gets ten shillings for them. She said I could have this one if I liked, but you wouldn't let me change the basket."

"Oh, darling, I didn't know you wanted a kitten so much!" said Mummy. "What a pity! I'm afraid we can't change the basket now."

"Well, Elsie, you are a goose," said Daddy suddenly. "You really are a *goose*. What about *my* birthday present to you? Have you forgotten it?"

"No, Daddy," said Elsie, surprised. "It was ten shillings to spend on myself."

"And how much did you say this kitten was?" asked Daddy.

"Ten shillings," said Elsie, and she suddenly stopped in the middle of the pavement and clapped her hands for joy. "Oh, Daddy! Ten shillings! I could *buy* the kitten myself with your present to me. Can I?"

"Of course," said Daddy. "Can't she, Mummy?"

"Yes," said Mummy, pleased. "So, Elsie, instead of taking the kitten back to leave it at the shop, we'll go and *buy* it!"

You should have seen Elsie's face! It was shining all over with joy! She had Daddy's ten shillings safely in her purse, so she could buy the kitten at once.

The shop-woman *was* surprised when she heard what Daddy had to say about the kitten.

"Hidden inside the work-basket!" she cried. "Well, what a very strange thing! I hunted all over the place last night for the little thing, and I couldn't find it anywhere. It must have wanted to go and live with Elsie."

"It *does* want to," said Elsie eagerly. "So may I buy it? It's my birthday today and Daddy has given me ten shillings. Here it is. May I take the kitten home again now?"

"Certainly," said the shop-woman, smiling. "But wait a minute — if it's your birthday I'd like to give you a little present, too. Look, here is a nice little round basket for your kitten to sleep in. It's the one she has been used to, so she will love it."

"Oh, thank you!" cried Elsie in delight. "This is the very nicest birthday I've ever had! I shall *love* that little white kitten. I shall call it Snowball, and play with it all the day long!"

So she does — and you should see Snowball now! She is the fattest, prettiest, naughtiest kitten you ever saw, but everyone loves her. Mummy often tells people how Snowball hid herself in Elsie's work-basket because she wanted to live with Elsie, and the listening kitten pricks up its ears and says: "Miaow! Miaow!" Which means, "Quite right! I meant to get what I wanted, and I got it!"

Jimmy wanted to go to the circus. All his friends were going – but somehow his Mummy and Daddy couldn't be bothered to take him. Mummy wasn't very well, and Daddy seemed very busy.

"I don't like to bother them," thought Jimmy to himself. "They will only get cross with me. But, dear me, how I wish I could go!"

"Jimmy! Jimmy! I want you to run an errand for me!" called Mummy. "Hurry, now! Go to Mrs. Brown's and tell her I want twelve new-laid eggs tomorrow."

Jimmy put down his engine and ran off. He went down the street, up the lane, over the hill, down to the farm, and all the way back again. It was a long walk, and Jimmy felt quite tired by the time he reached his own street once more.

And just as he turned into his street, he saw an old lady sitting on a doorstep, crying! This was such a surprising sight that Jimmy stood still and stared for a moment, quite forgetting that it isn't kind to stare. But he didn't think that grown-ups ever cried.

"What's the matter?" he said to the old lady, going up to her. "Don't you feel well?"

"I've lost my purse with all my money in it," said the old woman wiping her eyes with a big white handkerchief. "And there's my son's watch in it, too, that has just been mended. He will be so cross with me!"

"Where do you think you lost your purse?" asked

Jimmy, looking all round as if he expected to see it in the road somewhere.

"I've just come back from Mrs. Brown's at the farm," said the old lady. "I must have dropped it somewhere on the way."

"How funny!" said Jimmy. "I've just been to Mrs. Brown's, too – but I didn't see your purse on the way back. Of course, I was running, and not looking."

"I suppose you wouldn't go back and see if you can find it for me, little boy?" asked the old lady.

Jimmy didn't want to at all. He had already been all the way there and back, and he was tired and wanted to sit down with his book. It would be horrid to have to go to the farm again. But the old lady looked very sad, and he didn't like to think of someone as old as his Granny sitting on a doorstep and crying like that.

"I'll go and find it for you," he said. "You go home and sit down. I'll bring you the purse if I find it. Where do you live?"

"Number six in the next street," said the old lady, getting up. "Thank you kindly, little boy."

She walked slowly down the street, and Jimmy went back down the lane, looking everywhere for the purse. He kicked up the leaves, he looked under the hedges – but he couldn't find that purse anywhere in the lane. He went up the hill and looked there. He went almost to the farm, hunting all the way – and just as he got to the first farm-gate he saw the purse! It was a big brown one, lying in the mud! How pleased Jimmy was to see it!

He picked it up and ran off at once. His legs were really very tired by this time, but he felt so pleased about the purse that he didn't think of that!

He went to number six in the next street to his, and knocked.

"Come in!" cried a voice. Jimmy went in. The old lady was sitting down by a bright fire, drinking a cup of cocoa.

"I've found your purse!" said Jimmy, and he put it into her lap. "Wasn't that lucky?"

The old woman picked it up and opened it. She nodded her head. "Yes," she said, "all my money's there – and my son's watch, too. Now, little boy, would you be so kind as to take this watch to my son for me? I'm too tired to go out again, and he wants it tonight."

Well, Jimmy thought, that was too bad! To go out again! But, never mind, he'd do it! He took the watch from the old lady, asked her where he was to take it, and went out. Before he did anything more he ran home to tell his mother what had happened to him. She was getting quite worried about him.

"Well, Jimmy, you've been very kind to the old lady," she said. "Did she give you a penny or a bun, or something, to show you she was grateful?"

"No, Mummy," said Jimmy. "I expect she couldn't afford to give me anything – and, anyway, I didn't want anything. I didn't like to see her crying."

He went off with the watch. He had to take it to a house not very far away. He knocked at the door and asked for Mr. Siglio. That was the name of the old lady's son.

"He's upstairs," said the woman who opened the door. "You'll just catch him. He's off to his elephants in a minute!"

"His elephants!" said Jimmy, in surprise. "What do you mean?"

"Oh, he's the man that makes the elephants do their tricks at the circus," said the woman. "Didn't you know? Yes, he has eight fine elephants, and they all love him as if he were their brother! You should see how they twine their trunks round him and fuss him! Ah, you can see that man's been kind to his beasts!"

Mr. Siglio sounded rather a nice man, Jimmy thought. He went up the stairs and knocked on another door. He went in and there was the famous Mr. Siglio, dressing himself in bright-blue trousers, a yellow coat, and a great blue top-hat, just as he appeared in his circus pictures, that were posted all over the town.

"Hallo, hallo!" said Mr. Siglio, looking at Jimmy. "And who have we here? Mr. Tickle-me-up – or Master Tumble-me-down?"

"No," said Jimmy. "My name's Jimmy, and I've brought you your watch. I saw your mother sitting on a doorstep and crying because she had lost her purse with her money in it and your watch, too. I was lucky enough to find her purse, and she asked me to bring you the watch. So here it is!"

"And very kind of you, too," said Mr. Siglio, taking the watch and stuffing it into his trousers pocket. "What can I do for you in return?"

"Oh, nothing, thank you," said Jimmy. "I hope your elephants perform well tonight."

"Have you seen them at the circus?" asked Mr. Siglio.

"No," said Jimmy. "I haven't been, and I'm afraid I'm not going either."

"Bless us all!" said Mr. Siglio, putting his blue top-hat on his head, all on one side. "Here's a boy who hasn't seen my famous elephants! I can't allow this! Run home, boy, and tell your mother that Mr. Siglio, the famous elephant man, wants you to help him at the circus tonight!"

And that night Jimmy went to the circus – and will you believe it, Mr. Siglio got him into the big ring and made

He had never had such an exciting time

him help with the elephants. Yes, you could have seen Jimmy riding on one – and throwing a ball to another – and giving a bun to a third! He had never had such an exciting time in his life!

"I didn't know that old lady's son was Mr. Siglio, the famous elephant man," he told his father that night.

"Ah!" said his father, "there's a lot we don't know, Jimmy, till we give a bit of help to somebody. It's wonderful the things that happen then!"

The Enchanted Wheelbarrow

Once upon a time a gnome, called Tiptap, came to live in Snapdragon Village. He took the little cottage right at the end of the village, and there he lived by himself. He wasn't very friendly with the people round about him, and he didn't seem to do any work at all.

The reason was that he had an enchanted wheelbarrow. He had seen it hanging in a shop, and, being rather cleverer than most gnomes, he had known that it was enchanted. So he had bought it and taken it home. He had soon found out what it could do – and it was really very strange.

That wheelbarrow could set out by itself at midnight, wheeling along on its one wheel just as if someone was pushing it. And it could bring home anything that Tiptap wanted! Fancy that!

So, you see, he didn't need to buy any food or any clothes. When he wanted some breakfast bacon, or a big packet of chocolate, or a treacle pudding, he would dance round the barrow slowly, three times one way and three times the other, calling out the name of the thing he wanted.

Then, as the village clock struck twelve, that strange barrow would lift itself up and go trundling away on its one wheel. Tiptap never knew where it went. But it always came back with what he wanted – a big piece of breakfast bacon, or a packet of milk chocolate, or a steaming-hot treacle pudding. It was wonderful.

He got all his clothes in that way, and also a new clock, a gramophone, a canary in a cage, and a new hearth-rug. He didn't tell anyone about the magic in his barrow, so nobody could think how it was that, although Tiptap did no work, he always had plenty of food to eat and lots of nice things to wear.

Now one day, when Tiptap was out for a walk, he came to a little yellow cottage with pretty blue curtains at the window. Someone was singing inside the cottage, and Tiptap stopped to listen. The door was open, and inside Tiptap saw a very curious chair. It was made of some dark wood, and was carved all over with little animals.

It really was a lovely chair. Tiptap wanted it as soon as he saw it. So he went up the little path and knocked at the door. The singing stopped, and a pixie came to the door, wiping her hands on a cloth, for she had been doing her washing.

"Good morning," she said. "What can I do for you, Tiptap? You don't often come to see people!"

"No, I don't," said Tiptap. "But this morning I caught sight of that lovely carved chair of yours, and I like it so much I want you to sell it to me. I don't mind what money you ask me for it. I *must* have that chair."

"Well, I'm sorry, but you can't have it," said the pixie. "My great-great-great-great-great-grandfather carved it

66

for my great-great-great-great-great-grandmother, and so it has always been in our family, and we love it."

"What nonsense!" said Tiptap crossly. "If it's been in your family all that time I should think you must be tired of it. Sell it to me, please."

But Flip, the pixie, wouldn't sell it. She shut the door at last, and left Tiptap standing angrily on the doorstep.

He went home sulkily, thinking about that dear little carved chair, wondering how to make Flip sell it to him. And then an idea came into his head – a very naughty plan indeed. He would send his enchanted wheelbarrow to fetch it!

So that night Tiptap danced solemnly round the barrow, three times each way, calling out: "Flip's carved chair! Flip's carved chair!"

When the village clock began to strike midnight, the barrow lifted itself up and trundled off on its little wheel. Down the street it went, and up the crooked lane where Flip lived. It wheeled itself up the little path and then set itself silently down.

A curious blue light began to shine over the barrow. It was the magic working. At the same time there came a little sound from inside the sleeping cottage. It was the carved chair moving. The magic was calling it out.

The door opened and the chair slid out very quietly. The door shut. The chair lifted itself into the barrow, and at once the blue light round the barrow faded away again. The barrow lifted itself up and once again trundled away down the lane, making no noise at all, except a tiny little squeak now and again, because the chair was rather heavy.

Tiptap was waiting excitedly in his kitchen. Would his barrow bring back the chair or not? What a wonderful thing if it did! It would serve Flip, the pixie, right for not selling him the chair when he asked her. Aha! He would teach people to say no to him!

Just then the barrow arrived at the door and Tiptap heard its little squeak. He ran to the door in excitement and flung it open. The barrow wheeled itself in and Tiptap saw that Flip's little carved chair was there! How pleased he was! He lifted out the chair and sat down in it. Oh, it was really the loveliest chair in the world! He could look at it for hours. He thought there really must be every animal and bird carved on it, there were so many.

"I mustn't leave it about for anyone to see," thought Tiptap. "If I do, people will know it is Flip's, and they might put me in prison. I will put it in a cupboard in the daytime, and only bring it out to sit on at night. Then I shall be safe."

So that is what he did. All day it stood in a big cupboard off the kitchen, and at night it was brought out and Tiptap sat in it and read his paper.

But, dear me, when Flip the pixie got up the next morning and missed her chair, she couldn't think *where* it had gone to! It had been in its place by the fire the night before, when she had gone to bed – and now it wasn't there any more! She hunted all through the house for it – but it certainly was gone.

Then she remembered how Tiptap the gnome had wanted to buy it from her the day before, and she felt sure he had stolen it. So off she went to his cottage. Tiptap was out and the cottage door was locked.

"Good!" thought Flip. "I will peep into all the windows and see where my chair is."

Now Tiptap had only two rooms in his cottage, a bedroom and a kitchen, and as they each had two windows, on opposite sides of the room, Flip was able to see all round the two rooms when she peeped in. But to her surprise the chair was nowhere to be seen! There was a bed in the bedroom, and a chair and wash-stand with a chest of drawers in the corner – but the chair wasn't *her* chair.

In the kitchen there was a round table, an armchair, a stool, and a dresser. And that was all. She couldn't see the big cupboard in the wall, where Tiptap had hidden her chair, because he had artfully pushed his dresser against it, so that the cupboard door was quite hidden!

She went away, puzzled and sorrowful, and Tiptap who was just coming down the street, saw her go. He guessed she had been peeping into his windows, and he grinned to himself to think how cleverly he had hidden the little carved chair.

The next thing that Tiptap wanted was a porridge bowl he saw at Mrs. Crumple's, the washerwoman. It was the only lovely thing the poor woman had, and she wouldn't part with it for anything, no matter how badly off she was.

It was made of cherry-wood, and round the rim ran a row of tiny cats, carved in the cherry-wood itself. It really was a most exciting bowl to have porridge in, and Tiptap felt sure he could eat twice as much porridge if he had a bowl like that.

But Mrs. Crumple wouldn't sell it, although he offered her ten pieces of gold for it. Tiptap was very angry, but as he went home he began to smile. Of course, he could send his wheelbarrow for it!

He did so, that very night. Off it went on its one little wheel and stopped outside Mrs. Crumple's. Her window was open, and as soon as the strange blue light began to shine over the barrow, the porridge bowl appeared at the window. It flew out and went to the barrow. The blue light faded, the barrow lifted itself up and off it trundled once more, back to Tiptap.

He was waiting for it, and on the stove he had some porridge cooking. He took the bowl out of the barrow, and ladled some porridge into it. Then he put some treacle on the porridge, poured some milk over it, and sat down to eat his supper out of Mrs. Crumple's lovely bowl. Porridge had never tasted so nice before, never! Tiptap looked at the little row of cats as he ate. He was sitting in Flip's chair, of course, but he didn't feel a bit ashamed of himself. No, he was too pleased to think he had got Mrs. Crumple's bowl, after all!

Poor Mrs. Crumple! When she missed her bowl she sat down and wept, because it really was the only nice thing she had. She couldn't find it anywhere. She, too, went and peeped into Tiptap's windows, but he had hidden the bowl away with the chair in the cupboard, and as the big dresser was in front of the cupboard, Mrs. Crumple couldn't see it, of course.

After that Tiptap sent his barrow to fetch anything he fancied that belonged to other people. He took Mr. Twinkle's best pewter teapot. He took Dame See-Saw's nice old red shawl with the long fringe. He took the Green Elf's pretty hearth-rug, the one she had made herself with a pattern of ducks all over it.

Of course, everyone in Snapdragon Village began to wonder where their things disappeared to – and they all felt quite certain that Tiptap had somehow or other taken them. So the very next time that Tiptap went to someone to ask them to sell him something, a watch was kept.

It happened that Tiptap saw a lovely old spoon at Binkie Brownie's, and at once he thought how nice it would be to use with his porridge bowl. Binkie Brownie said he wouldn't sell it – and as soon as Tiptap had gone home the brownie called a meeting.

"I'm sure Tiptap will steal my spoon tonight," he said.

"We'll watch for him, shall we? We'll all hide in my garden, behind the bushes – then when he comes creeping along we'll catch him!"

"Yes, and we'll make him tell where he has hidden all our things!" cried the others. So that night a great many of the folk of Snapdragon Village hid in Binkie's garden, and kept as quiet as mice, watching and listening.

Tiptap was in his kitchen, dancing solemnly round his barrow, three times this way and three times that, calling out. "Binkie Brownie's old spoon, Binkie Brownie's old spoon!" Then, as the clock struck twelve, off went the barrow once more, trundling down the street to the cottage where Binkie Brownie lived.

The little folk hiding in the bushes heard the barrow coming, and they wondered what it was. They peeped out of the bushes to see. When they saw a barrow wheeling itself along they were most astonished.

"Don't say a word!" whispered Binkie, in excitement. "We'll see what it does! Perhaps the barrow is the thief, not Tiptap!"

The little folk watched the barrow come to rest on the path outside the cottage. Then they saw the strange blue light shine over it, and they trembled, for they knew that powerful magic was at work. Then, to their enormous astonishment, the door opened and out flew Binkie's lovely old spoon, right into the barrow. The blue light faded away and off went the barrow down the street.

"Follow it!" whispered Binkie. So the little folk crept after it, and when they saw it go into Tiptap's garden gate, they knew that what they had thought before was quite true. Tiptap was the one who had really stolen their things.

They all went back to Binkie's and talked hard.

"I will get that barrow and have a look at it," said

71

Binkie. "It would be fun to use it to fetch Tiptap here, wouldn't it? We'll see what we can do. Leave it to me. Come here tomorrow night and we might see something funny happening!"

The next day Tiptap went to see his aunt who lived two villages away. So Binkie was easily able to visit his garden shed and have a look at his barrow. Just as he thought, it was an enchanted barrow. Binkie wheeled it off to his own house, grinning very widely indeed. Tiptap was going to get a shock that night!

Binkie showed the barrow to the others, and explained to them the magic that was in it.

"My old Uncle Wump had a barrow like this," he said. "So I know how it works. We'll play a fine trick on Tiptap tonight, the horrid little thief!"

So, just before midnight, Binkie Brownie danced solemnly round the barrow, three times one way and three times the other, crying: "Tiptap, Tiptap, Tiptap!" as he went. And as the clock struck twelve the barrow lifted itself up, and off it went on its one wheel, down the street to where the gnome lived.

Binkie and his friends waited excitedly in Binkie's cottage, wondering how long it would be before the barrow came back. It had gone to Tiptap's, and was standing outside the cottage. Tiptap was in bed and fast asleep. The blue light began to shine over the barrow as the magic worked – and, oh, my goodness me, Tiptap got the shock of his life!

He felt himself being pulled out of bed. The clothes were thrown off him, and although Tiptap held tightly to the mattress it wasn't a bit of use. He had to go. He was dragged to the door, which opened in front of him. Then he was pushed head over heels into the waiting barrow!

He sat in the barrow, wondering what was happening. It was dark and he didn't know he was in his barrow until it started to wheel itself down the street! Then he heard its little squeak and guessed where he was. He tried to jump out of the barrow, but he couldn't. He simply couldn't. The magic held him firmly there, and there he had to stay.

At last Binkie and his friends heard the little squeak of the barrow coming back again. It wheeled itself up the garden path and into the door of Binkie's cottage – and in it lay Tiptap, frightened out of his life, wondering how it was that he had been caught like this!

The barrow stopped inside Binkie's kitchen. Binkie and the others stared at Tiptap, and then Binkie spoke very sternly.

"So you are the robber, are you!" he said. "You're the thief who stole Flip's carved chair, Mrs. Crumple's porridge bowl, and all the other things! You're the one who sent your barrow here to steal my lovely old spoon. Ah, you're caught, you wicked robber – caught in your own barrow!"

Tiptap found that he could jump out of the barrow now. He sprang out and stood up straight.

"How dare you accuse me of stealing those things!" he cried. "I know nothing about them! Nothing, I tell you! Perhaps my barrow stole them, but *I* didn't! I expect the barrow took them, and then gave them to someone who knows about the magic in it."

"Well, we want to know where the things are, Tiptap," said Binkie sharply. "It's no use saying you didn't have them. Tell us where you have hidden them, and we'll get them back."

But Tiptap still went on saying that he hadn't stolen them, and he didn't know where the things were. So at last

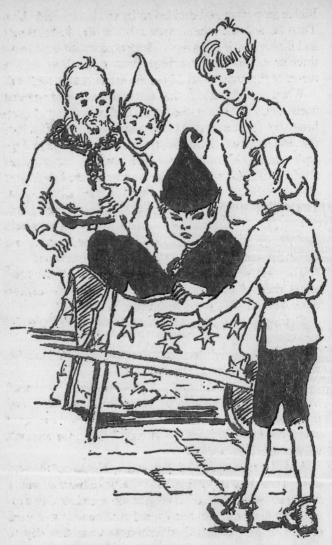

'So you are the robber, are you!' he said

Binkie gave it up and decided to let the barrow help him. Then he and the others made a list of the stolen things and Binkie took it in his hand. He danced round the barrow three times this way, and three times that, calling out the names of the stolen things, from the list he held in his hand.

When he had finished, the barrow tilted up and wheeled itself away. Everyone followed, Binkie holding Tiptap firmly by the arm, making him come along, too. The barrow wheeled itself down the street, and soon came to Tiptap's cottage. The door flew open and the barrow went inside. Then, to everyone's great surprise, the big dresser moved itself and showed a cupboard in the wall behind it. The door of the cupboard opened – and out came Flip's carved chair, Mrs. Crumple's porridge bowl, Mr. Twinkle's best pewter teapot, Dame See-Saw's nice red shawl, the Green Elf's hearth-rug, and Binkie's lovely old spoon!

They all flew to the wheelbarrow and arranged themselves there. Binkie and the others stared with surprise to see them all. What a wicked gnome Tiptap was!

"I suppose you'll say next you didn't put them there!" said Binkie.

But Tiptap knew it was no use saying that. He hung his head and grew red in the face.

"You are a wicked gnome," said Binkie. "You shall be spanked by each one of us whose things you took, and then you can get into your magic wheelbarrow and let it wheel you far away from Snapdragon Village, for we don't want people like *you* here!"

And, dear me, what a lot of spanking Tiptap got the next day! Then Binkie put him into the wheelbarrow, said a wise spell over it, and off it went at top speed, taking Tiptap away to goodness knows where! And nobody has heard of him or his enchanted wheelbarrow from that day to this.

Santa Claus Makes A Mistake

Ellen and Jack were very excited. It was Christmas Eve, and they meant to hang up their stockings at the end of their beds. Daddy had given each of them one of his big ones, and they were very pleased.

They hung them up and then jumped into bed. "You must go to sleep quickly," Mother said, "because, you know, Santa Claus won't come until you are fast asleep."

So Ellen and Jack shut their eyes and tried to go to sleep – and it wasn't very long before they were both fast asleep and dreaming. They slept and slept, whilst the clock struck eight – and nine – and ten – and eleven! All the grown-ups went to bed. The lights were turned out. The house was dark.

The dog slept on his rug. The cat slept in her basket. Everything was quiet – except the fire in the dining-room, which made a little noise now and again when the hot coals fell together.

Towards midnight Ellen woke up suddenly. She sat up in bed, wondering what had awakened her. The nursery was dark. Jack was fast asleep. She could hear him breathing.

She listened. She thought perhaps she might have been dreaming. She switched on the light and looked round the nursery. She looked at the end of the bed where she and Jack had hung their stockings. To her great disappointment they were quite empty.

"I wonder if that is because Santa Claus hasn't been yet," wondered Ellen. "Oh, how dreadful it will be if we find our stockings empty in the morning!"

Just as she was turning out the light she heard the noise again. It was a funny noise – a sort of scraping, kicking noise – and then she heard a deep groan.

"Goodness gracious, whatever can it be!" thought Ellen. She leaned over to Jack's bed and woke him up. The scraping noise went on and on. Jack sat up and asked Ellen what all the noise was about.

"Jack," said Ellen, "I can't help thinking it's someone stuck in the chimney downstairs! That's what it sounds like to me. Oh, Jack – do you suppose it's Santa Claus?"

"I say!" said Jack. "I say! Suppose it is! Suppose he's stuck! Come on quickly, Ellen, we must go and see."

The two children put on their dressing-gowns and slippers, pushed open their door and slipped down the stairs. They went into the dining-room and saw the little red fire there. They heard the dog growling in the kitchen, for he too had heard the strange noises.

"Look! Look!" said Ellen, pointing to the fireplace. "There's a boot hanging down the chimney! Look!"

Sure enough, there was a boot there – a big black boot – and it was on a leg – and the leg was kicking about! As the children watched, another boot came down the chimney.

"It *is* Santa Claus!" said Jack. "He always wears big black boots in his pictures. Oh, Ellen, he's come down the wrong chimney. He'll burn himself on the fire!"

"I'll put it out before he does," said Ellen at once. She turned on the light and went to the kitchen. She filled a jug at the tap and carried it back to the dining-room. She poured water on the fire.

77

Sizzle-sizzle-sizzle! The fire streamed up in a cloud of thick black smoke! A startled voice from the chimney said: "Hallo! Is anybody there? My word, this smoke is going to make me sneeze!"

"It's only Ellen and Jack," said Jack. "We know you are Santa Claus. We've put the fire out so that you won't get burnt. That is why it is smoking so much. We've just poured some water on it. You've come down the wrong chimney, Santa Claus."

"Dear, dear!" said Santa Claus. "Have I really? You know, I have a map showing the chimneys of every house, and the right ones, leading to the children's bedrooms, are marked with a yellow cross – and tonight the wind blew my map away so I had to guess! And I've guessed wrong! I'm stuck here."

"We could give you a pull," said Ellen. "Jack can take one leg and I can pull the other."

"Go on, then," said Santa Claus. So they each took hold of a black-booted leg and pulled hard. Santa Claus came down with a rush and sat in the fire-place! A big burly man in red, with a twinkling smile and the kindest eyes the children had ever seen.

"These coals are still hot!" said Santa Claus getting up in a hurry. "It's kind of you children to help me like this. Do you mind if I stay here for a little while till the reindeer I sent to look for my blown-away map comes back and gives it to me? I shall most likely make a few more mistakes if I go on guessing which are the right chimneys."

"Oh, Santa Claus, of course stay as long as you like," said Ellen. "We'd simply love you to. I'll got some of my chocolates for you."

"You don't suppose the grown-ups will wake up and hear me, do you?" whispered Santa Claus, suddenly remembering that there were other people in the house. "I never know what to say to grown-ups, you know. They make me shy. It's children I like."

"Oh, I don't think Mummy and Daddy will wake," said Ellen. "They sleep very soundly. And cook and Jane sleep at the top of the house. The only thing that might happen is that Spot, our dog, may bark."

"Well, go and bring him here," said Santa Claus. "I have a rubber bone for him, I think. It was down on my list – one dog, one rubber bone – and he might as well have it now. Dogs don't seem to hang stockings up, so I usually give them a present straight away or put it into their baskets if they are not awake."

Jack went to fetch Spot, who seemed most delighted to see Santa Claus. He jumped up on his knee and licked his face all over.

"His tongue is as good as a sponge!" said Santa Claus. "Here, Spot, lick this bone for a change. I really don't think my face want washing any more."

Jack and Ellen were so happy. It was the greatest adventure in the world to be sitting with Santa Claus, hearing him talk and laugh, and seeing him eat their chocolates.

Suddenly there came a little soft knocking at the window. Santa Claus jumped up. "That's my reindeer come back!" he said.

He opened the window softly – and, to the children's enormous surprise, a big furry head was pushed in! It was the head of one of the reindeer. Its antlers were so big that they could not get inside the window, so the reindeer could only put in its big, soft nose, so long and velvety. In its mouth it held a large piece of paper.

"Thanks, reindeer," said Santa Claus, and he rubbed its nose. "I'm glad to get my map back again. Have you

Santa Claus came down with a rush

got a bit of sugar for the old fellow, children?"

"Of course!" said Ellen, and she ran to the sideboard where the basin of sugar was kept. She took out a handful of sugar lumps and she and Jack fed the delighted reindeer. Then Santa Claus shut the window and looked at the map. It was a most curious map, showing nothing but chimneys, and the page was marked with scores of yellow crosses.

"Well, my dears," said Santa Claus, with a sigh, rolling up his map, "I must be off! I have so much enjoyed this little time with you – nice, kind creatures children are! I always did like them much better than grown-ups. I'm a bit late now, because of losing this map, so I must be off. Thanks so much for your help, and the chocolates, and the sugar lumps. Do you mind letting me out of the front door? I don't like to try that chimney again, you know."

The children took Santa Claus to the front door and let him out. He gave them each a hug and disappeared into the night. They heard him whistling to his reindeer, and listened to the jingling of the sleigh-bells as the reindeer moved up to Santa Claus.

Ellen and Jack shut the door and went up to bed. They were so excited that they could not go to sleep.

"I'm afraid we shan't have any presents in our stockings, Ellen," said Jack. "Santa Claus won't come here now."

"Well, I don't mind," said Ellen. "I've *seen* him – and spoken to him – and fed his reindeer – and given him a hug! I don't care if he never fills my stockings again! He's real, and I've seen him!"

It was a long time before the children did at last fall asleep. And you know, in the morning when they sat up in bed – their stockings were fuller than they had ever been before! And there were presents on the bed and on the floor, too!

"He *did* come back again!" said Ellen, in delight. "Oh, the darling! Look what's in our stockings, Jack – the loveliest toys we've ever had!"

"Now don't say a word to anyone about us seeing Santa Claus last night, and pulling him down the chimney," said Jack. "He'd like us to keep it a secret, I know. Fancy him coming back again to our house – and getting the chimney right this time!"

Daddy and Mummy were *so* surprised to see what a lot of things the children had in their stockings and on the bed. "It was a good thing you were asleep when he came," said Mummy. "He doesn't like children to see him, you know."

She couldn't *think* why Ellen and Jack looked at one another and smiled, when she said that – but I know why, don't you?

The King's Hairbrush

Once upon a time there was a King who had a wonderful hairbrush. His name was Rumbledy, and he ruled over Ho-Ho Land, where the yellow pixies live. He had bought his hairbrush from the Moon-Witch, and people say that he paid her a hundred glittering diamonds for it.

The King had straight hair – very straight indeed; but as soon as he used the magic hairbrush, hey presto, his hair curled beautifully all over his head! Then how handsome he looked! His Queen praised him and his courtiers rushed for their cameras at once. He certainly looked very nice.

Now the King didn't tell anyone, not even his Queen, about his new hairbrush. Everyone though his hair had suddenly turned curly, and they told him he was very lucky. The King kept his brush locked up in a drawer, and he only took it out once each twenty-four hours, and that was at ten o'clock at night, just before he went to bed.

He had to use his magic brush once each night, or his hair became as straight as ever. So he would sit on his bed and brush his hair ten times – and then he would know that his hair would be curly the next day for certain sure.

Now one night King Rumbledy quite forgot to draw the blinds before he sat down on the bed to brush his hair. He was tired that night, for he had been to a party, and it was almost midnight. The King never liked to stay out after midnight for at twelve o'clock his hair always went straight again. It lost its magic then.

Rumbledy yawned and took off his crown. He slipped his arms out of his gold and silver coat and threw it on the bed. He could hear the Queen splashing in her bath, so he thought he would take out his hairbrush from the locked drawer and brush his hair before she came to bed.

Just as he took it from his drawer, the big clock in the palace hall struck midnight. It said "Dong" very loudly twelve times – and as the last stroke died away the King's hair lost its curls and became as straight as could be! How different he looked!

Now out in the palace garden was Longnose, a pixie, who was most inquisitive. He always wanted to poke his long nose into everything. He loved to peep through key-holes, he liked to look into everyone's windows, and he loved to find out secrets. He was a most unpleasant fellow.

Longnose was in the palace garden because he had seen a light in the King's bedroom, and had noticed that the blinds were not drawn. He had jumped over the palace wall, and had crept up underneath the window. Then he climbed up a tree whose branches tapped against the window and peeped into the bedroom to see what he could see.

"Perhaps I shall see if the King uses a gold tooth-brush or not," he said to himself. "What a bit of news to tell my friends, if he does! Or perhaps I shall hear him snore."

But what Longnose did see was far more exciting than anything he had thought of!

He saw King Rumbledy go to a drawer and take out a brush – and then Longnose suddenly noticed that the King's hair was straight – just as straight as could be, so that the King looked quite different. Then, when Rumbledy brushed his hair with the little yellow hairbrush, hey presto! His hair curled up again as tight as could be, and was perfectly lovely!

"So that's how he gets his curls," thought Longnose. "Well, well! What a bit of news!"

The King popped the hairbrush down on a table by the window and bent to look at his hair in the glass. Then a wicked thought came to Longnose. He slipped his hand in at the window, took up the hairbrush without the King seeing him, and hopped down the tree as fast as ever he could!

He ran down the palace garden and climbed over the wall as quick as lightening. Then off he went to his little cottage in the wood, holding the hairbrush tightly in his hand.

He lighted a candle when he was safely inside the cottage. He looked carefully at the little yellow brush. It seemed quite ordinary – but it wasn't! Ah, Longnose knew what magic lay in that small brush!

He looked in the glass. His hair was straight and greasy. He would brush it well and let it grow curly like the King's. How good-looking he would be then!

So he brushed his hair with the magic hairbrush – and, hey presto, how his long hair curled! It bunched itself tightly round his head, and Longnose looked quite different. He was very pleased. He put the brush down on a table and looked at himself with delight.

And then a queer thing happened. The yellow hairbrush suddenly jumped up from the table and rapped him hard on the knuckles! Then it leapt into the air and vanished! At least, Longnose *thought* it had vanished – it hadn't really. It had just flown up the chimney and stayed there, angry because someone had used it who had no business to.

Longnose looked for it and then gave it up. Most delighted with his curly hair, he got into bed and fell asleep. But in the night he awoke to feel something very queer happening up him. Something was gently brushing his long nose!

It was the brush. It had come down from the chimney and was brushing Longnose's nose. When it felt the pixie waking up, it fled back to the chimney again.

Longnose sneezed twice and fell asleep once more – but, oh, my goodness me, when he got up the next morning and looked in the glass, what did he see? The most peculiar-looking nose he had ever come across in his life!

It was curly! Yes, really. The brush had brushed it, and it had curled itself round like a corkscrew. Longnose looked very queer. His hair was curly too, but that looked all right. It was his nose that looked so dreadful.

"Oh, my goodness me!" cried Longnose, in dismay. "Look at my nose! Whatever am I to do? I can't possibly go out like this! Everyone will laugh at me."

He tried to pull his nose straight, but he couldn't. It wouldn't go straight. It was as curly as could be. When he took out his handkerchief and blew his nose, it made a noise like a big trumpet. It was dreadful, and Longnose wept big tears for a whole hour.

He decided that he wouldn't go out that day, then nobody would see him. So, although the sun was shining beautifully, Longnose stayed indoors, hardly daring to look at himself in the glass. He wondered and wondered where the brush had gone to, but he never once thought of looking up the chimney.

He went to bed a very sad little pixie that night – and, oh, dear me, in the middle of the night the brush came down from its hiding-place and woke Longnose up again! This time it brushed his long, pointed ears, and Longnose lay trembling in bed, not daring to move.

In the morning his ears had gone all curly! You should have seen them! They looked very queer. Longnose groaned when he saw them – and then he saw that his hair had gone straight again, for, you know, it needed to be

86

brushed each night with the magic brush, if it was to keep curly. But his nose was still as curly as ever. The magic had stayed in that.

"How I wish I hadn't been so sly, peeping in at the King's window," wept Longnose. "It serves me right. But what am I to do? I can't keep indoors for ever. Besides, I shall soon have to go out shopping and get some things in to eat. I've hardly any bread left, and no butter at all."

Now all this time the King had been wondering and wondering where his hairbrush had gone. He had hunted for it everywhere, and made the Queen quite cross, because she didn't know what he was looking for, and he wouldn't tell her.

When the second night came and still there was no brush to be found, the King was most upset. He knew that his hair would be as straight as a poker the next day. But it wasn't a bit of good – he couldn't find that brush anywhere. And no wonder, because it was hiding safely up the chimney of Longnoses's cottage!

The poor King couldn't keep his secret any longer. He awoke the next morning with his hair in long, straight tresses, falling to his shoulders. He looked dreadful. He called the royal barber to him and commanded him to cut his hair short. The man stared in the greatest surprise at the King's straight hair. When he had finished cutting it, he rushed out and told all his friends what he had done.

Then the King sent his heralds out, for he meant to get his hairbrush back. They set out on horseback, blowing silver trumpets, and reading from big sheets of parchment.

"Oyez, oyez, the King offers a great reward to anyone who will return his lost yellow hairbrush, which has the power of making the hair curl. Oyez, Oyez!"

What a chattering there was all over the kingdom! How

everyone hunted and searched! But nobody could find that brush.

Now there was a small pixie called Dumpling, who lived next door to Longnose. He was a kind-hearted little fellow, and when he didn't see Longnose coming out to shop, or running into his garden to hang up clothes, he wondered it he was ill.

So he went to knock at the door and ask Longnose.

"Go away,' said Longnose, from indoors. "I'm all right. Go away."

Dumpling went away, but he couldn't help wondering why Longnose sounded so cross.

"He *must* be ill!" thought Dumpling. "Well, I'll just make him one of my famous raspberry jellies, and put it in the kitchen window without a word. He can eat it if he wants to.

So he made a jelly, and as soon as it was set he crept into Longnose's back garden. He went to the kitchen window and peeped in, meaning to put the jelly on the table that stood just inside the window.

And, oh, dear, he saw Longnose sitting by the fire – but *was* it Longnose? *Could* it be Longnose? What a dreadful curly nose! And oh, those awful curly ears! Whatever had happened? Dumpling gave a frightened shriek, dropped the jelly on his toes, and fled away.

He went back to his own cottage and sat down to think – and suddenly he knew what had happened to poor Longnose. The naughty pixie had somehow got hold of the magic hairbrush, and by some mistake his nose and ears had become curly!

"Poor Longnose," said Dumpling, shaking his head. "No wonder he won't come out of doors. I will go to the King and tell him what I know, and maybe he will go to

Longnose and make him say where the brush is, and cure his nose and ears."

So he told King Rumbledy, and the King at once set out for Longnose's cottage. Rat-tat-tat! He knocked at the door, and, then, without waiting for Longnose to say "come in", he walked straight in!

The pixie jumped up in fright; when he saw the King before him he nearly fell flat with fear and astonishment.

"How did you get your curly nose and ears?" asked the King sternly.

Longnose began to stutter and stammer, and at last he told how he had peeped in at the King's window and seen him use the magic brush. The King listened to him with a frown.

Then he clapped his hands three times and said: "Where are you, brush? Come out with a rush!"

At once the hairbrush rushed down the chimney and fell into the King's hand. How pleased he was to see it! He turned to go – but Longnose pulled at his arm.

"Your Majesty. What about *me*? Can you make my nose and ears straight again? Oh, please, please do!"

"Longnose," said the King sternly, "I have heard of you and your sly, interfering ways, always peeping and prying. I *could* make your nose and ears right again, but I'm not going to. They will get straight by themselves as soon as you get out of your horrid habits of peeping and prying – but if you forget and become deceitful again, you will find them becoming curly – so beware!"

Poor Longnose! He cried and cried when the King had gone. He *had* to go out shopping, and he didn't know what he would do when people pointed their fingers at him and laughed.

But he had to put up with it. It was all his own fault.

Dumpling gave a frightened shriek

"I'll never, never poke my nose into other people's business again!" vowed Longnose. "This had been a terrible lesson to me!"

So he stopped peeping and prying into other people's affairs – and gradually his nose became straight again, and his ears lost their curliness. He is nearly all right now, so I expect in the end he will become quite a nice fellow.

Dumpling got the reward, which was half a sack of gold. He bought a cow, a sheep, and a goat, and he is very happy looking after them. The King brushes his hair once more each night with the magic hairbrush, and now his hair is as curly as ever, so *he's* quite happy too. *I'd* like to use that brush just once, wouldn't you?

The Tiger and the Rabbit

As the splendid tiger was wandering through the jungle one day, a little sandy rabbit hopped out of a hole in front of him. The rabbit was so terrified at seeing the great tiger near at hand, that he sat there unable to move.

The tiger put his great paw down on the rabbit and held him.

"Mercy, mercy!" squealed the rabbit. "Let me free, great tiger! Oh, mercy, mercy! If you will let me go I will repay you one day!"

"Ho!" said the tiger scornfully. "How can a poor creature like you do a good turn to a tiger?"

"I might save your life, Master!" cried the rabbit eagerly. "You cannot tell. Oh, great and excellent tiger, braver and stronger than King Lion himself, let me go! I will save your life some day, that I promise you! You have only to roar for me and I will come from my burrow like the wind!"

"Well," said the tiger, taking his big paw from the trembling rabbit, "you may go! I have had my dinner, and do not need a small mouthful like you. I will see if you keep your word – but you rabbits are poor creatures, timid and foolish. You couldn't help a mouse, and as for a tiger – well – it is almost impertinent to think of such a thing!"

The rabbit did not wait for a moment, fearful lest the tiger should change him mind and gobble him up. He darted into his burrow and sat there shivering, thinking over and over again of what a narrow escape he had had. His heart was full of gratitude to the merciful tiger, and he longed to show him some kindness in return.

The tiger forgot all about the rabbit. He hunted throughout the week, and ate well. He slept in a close thicket of trees and bushes during the hot daytime, and sometimes was so well fed that he slept half the night as well.

He stole cattle from a native village. First one fat cow he took, and then another. The natives were angry and afraid. They made up their minds to set a trap for the tiger. They found the path he used each night to the cattle enclosure, and in the middle of that they dug a very deep pit.

It was wide as well as deep. Then, to prevent the tiger from scraping a foothold in the walls to spring out of the pit, they rammed the cut trunks of trees closely together all around the pit.

On the top they placed a loose platform of sticks, laid across from side to side, and covered with leaves and grass to look as if it were part of the path.

"Ha!" said the natives, pleased with their work. "This is a fine trap! Once the tiger treads on the top of it he will fall down into the pit with a crash. It is too deep for him to leap from, and because it is lined with timbers he cannot scrape footholds in the sides! We shall catch him tonight!"

They were right! The tiger came padding along that night, and when he trod on the loose platform of leaves and sticks, it gave way beneath his weight, and he fell with a crash into the pit.

How angry he was! How he roared! How he scraped at the timbers lining the pit – but they were too well placed to give way. The tiger was caught. He could not jump out, for the pit was too deep. There he must stay until the natives came the next morning and killed him with spears.

The tiger would not lie still. He paced round and round the great pit, and every now and again he lifted his great head and roared into the night. The natives shook to hear him. Someone else heard him, too – the little rabbit whose life he had spared.

"It is my friend the tiger asking for me!" cried the rabbit, and he set off at top speed to the pit. When he reached it, he peered down at the furious tiger.

"Friend!" he cried. "I come to help you!"

The tiger looked at him in scorn.

"Ho, the foolish rabbit again! Well, rabbit, and how are you going to get me out of this! Ah, for all your grand promises, you are nothing but a silly, timid creature, of no use to a royal beast like myself! Go away and leave me to myself."

The rabbit hopped down fearlessly into the pit and looked all around it. He saw the timbers rammed tightly against the wall, and, as his bright eyes roved round, an idea came into his head.

"Sir!" he said to the tiger. "Master! I can set you free! I will get my friends to help me. Do not despair!"

To the tiger's great surprise the rabbit hopped up the side of the pit and disappeard into the night.

But he was soon back again, this time with about fifty rabbits like himself, all rather scared, but determined to do what their friend asked them.

The rabbit made ten hop down into the pit with him, the tiger first promising that he would not hurt any of them. The rest began to burrow swiftly outside the pit, down, down, down into the earth.

The tiger watched the rabbits inside the pit scornfully. He had no faith in such silly creatures! What were they going to do? If *he* could not get out of the pit with all his strength, surely they did not think *they* could get him out.

The rabbits inside the pit began to gnaw hard at one of the tree-trunks. Their sharp teeth bit right through the bark, right into the heart of the tree. Gnaw, gnaw, gnaw! How they bit into the timber, and very soon the tiger saw that they had bitten the trunk right in half. Then they set to work on the same tree-trunk, but a good bit lower down. Soon they had taken out a large piece from the trunk, and it fell to the bottom of the pit with a crash. Then they set to work on the next piece of timber.

When they had bitten big pieces out of five pieces of timber, the tiger heard a curious scraping sound on the other side of the pit wall. It was all the other rabbits burrowing nearer and nearer to the pit! They had dug an enormous hole, working hard with their strong feet, and had tunnelled downwards to the side of the pit – just to where the inside rabbits had bitten out the pieces of tree-trunks! Soon they made a hole right into the pit itself, and crawled through the space left where the tree-trunks had been bitten through.

"Now, Master," said the rabbit in excitement, "can you crawl into this space in the pit wall between the timbers we have bitten, and escape through the big tunnel we have made?"

Of course he could! It didn't take a moment for the tiger to squeeze through and make his way up the big tunnel that all the rabbits had made for him. Soon he stood in the open air again, glad to be free. "Good night, Master!" called the rabbit. "I said I would repay you for your mercy to me! I have done so!"

Off they went to their burrows and the tiger bounded gladly away to the jungle. As for the natives next day when they came to the pit, how amazed they were to find the timbers that lined the pit bitten through, and a great tunnel leading out of it.

"It was no tiger we caught!" they cried. "It must have been a MONSTROUS rabbit!"

Peeky and the Tools

There was once a small boy called Ian, who had a great many uncles and aunts. He was very lucky because they were kind people, and gave him all sorts of presents. You should have seen his cupboard! It was crammed so full that the toys overflowed on to the floor.

His bookshelf was full of lovely picture books, and he had a puppy and a kitten of his own. He had a splendid motor-car that he could work by pedals, and that had a horn almost as loud as his Daddy's. He really was lucky.

But he was a careless little boy. He didn't care for his toys at all. He really had too many. He broke them, he lost them, he tore them, and he left them out in the rain. His mother was always scolding him for treating his things so badly, but it didn't make a bit of difference.

There was one thing Ian hadn't got, which he simply LONGED to have – and that was a box of tools – real tools that he could make things with. He begged his Daddy to buy him some, but Daddy shook his head.

"No, Ian," he said. "You are much too careless with your belongings. A good box of tools costs a lot of money, and I know what you would do with them – leave them out in the rain! Then they would all get rusty and be of no use at all."

Ian went very red, but he knew what his Daddy said was quite true. He would have to do without his tools. But would you believe it – the very next day his Uncle Peter came to see him and brought him the loveliest box of tools you ever saw!

There was a great big hammer; a little hammer; a screw-driver; a plane; two saws; a chisel; a gimlet; a pair of pincers; a bag of screws; and a bag of nails. What do you think of that? They were all in a lovely oak box, and on the lid was carved Ian's name – Ian Harrison.

The little boy was so delighted. He hugged his uncle and thanked him.

"Now mind you take care of those," said Uncle Peter. "They are good tools, and you mustn't let them get rusty."

Ian promised that he would take great care of them. Daddy said he would get him some wood so that he could make something with his new tools.

The next day Ian began carpentering. You should have seen him hammer! You should have heard him sawing! My goodness me, he *did* work hard! And that day when he had finished, he put his tools carefully away in the box, after wiping them with an oily rag, just as Daddy had shown him.

The next day he went carpentering again, but this time he put the tools away without wiping them over carefully. He had lost the rag!

The next day he threw his tools into the box and forgot to shut the lid down. And after that he didn't take any care of them at all, but just left them lying about as he left everything else.

And that was how Peeky the gnome found them. Peeky was sad because he had had a great disappointment that day. He was going to marry Tippy the elf, and she had promised to live in the old hollow tree with him if he would make it really nice inside. She wanted four chairs, a round table, a stool, and a cupboard there. Peeky could make them all quite well, but he had no tools.

But he knew where to borrow them. He had a brother over in Bluebell Village who would lend all the tools he needed. So he started off to ask him – and, when he got there, what a dreadful disappointment he had! His brother had moved away from the village and taken all his tools with him!

So Peeky walked all the way back, feeling most miserable. And then he found Ian's tools!

There they were, lying out on the grass, just where the careless boy had left them. It was raining hard and they were all wet. Peeky stood still and looked at them in surprise.

Then the tools spoke to him.

"Little gnome!" said the hammer, in a curious knocking voice, "put us in shelter, out of the rain, will you?"

"Please do!" said the saw, in a grating voice. "I shan't be any use if I get much rustier. In fact, I believe I'm rusty now."

"You are," said Peeky. "You want rubbing over well, or you'll never saw again."

"And we shan't be any use as screws or nails soon!" cried the nails anxiously. "The rain is wetting us!"

"Who do you belong to?" asked Peeky.

"We belong to Ian, who is always leaving us about," said the big hammer. "He is a perfect nuisance."

"Well, shall I take you to my home and wipe you dry?"

asked Peeky. "You're very wet."

"Oh, please do!" cried all the tools together.

So Peeky picked up all the tools, held them under his coat to keep them from the wet, and went off to his hollow tree. He had a little stove lighted there, and he put all the tools round it in the warmth. They were delighted.

When they were quite dry, Peeky picked them up and saw how rusty some of them were getting. So he got some rough paper and scoured them well with it. Then he took an oily rag and rubbed them up and down with that. You should have seem them then! They shone like silver, they looked as if they were longing to do some work!

"I wish you were mine," said Peeky sadly. "I badly want some good tools like you to make four chairs, a round table, a stool, and a cupboard, for Tippy the elf, who is going to marry me. But I haven't any tools, and my brother, who could have lent me some, has gone away."

"Well, Peeky," said the big hammer, in its queer knocking voice. "Use us if you like! Why not let us make for you all the things you want? That nasty, careless boy, Ian, won't miss us, *I* can tell you! He would probably have left us out in the rain for a week! And, anyhow, even if he *does* miss us, it will give him a fright and serve him right!"

"Oh, do you think I really might borrow you?" cried Peeky, in delight. "What fun! How lucky I shall be to have good tools like you working for me! When shall we begin? Tomorrow?"

"Certainly!" shouted all the tools together, and the nails and screws jingled excitedly. "We will do our very best for you!"

So the next day Peeky and the tools set to work together. Peeky had plenty of good wood and the tools hammered, sawed, planed, and chiselled gaily. They made two lovely chairs that day and started on a third, so you can guess how hard they worked. And at the end of the day Peeky polished up the tools carefully, and put them in a nice dry place. He knew that good tools needed good care.

"I wonder if Ian has missed you yet," he said to the tools.

Yes, Ian had! What do you think had happened? Why, after tea on the day that he had left them out in the rain, who should come to see him again but his Uncle Peter who had given him the tools!

"Hallo, Ian," said Uncle Peter. "What about those fine tools I gave you last time? What have you made with them?"

"Well – nothing much," said Ian. "I began two or three things, and then I got tired of them before I finished them."

"What a pity!" said Uncle Peter. "Where are the tools? Have you kept them nice and bright, as I told you to?"

Ian went red.

"Y-y-y-y-y-yes," he stammered, not liking to say that he had kept them very badly. Daddy saw how red he had gone, and knew by the way that he stammered that something was not quite right.

"You had better fetch Uncle Peter your tools and show him whether you have kept them carefully or not," he said sternly.

Ian ran out of the room. He felt hot and bothered, and rather frightened. Where had he left those tools? He had had them in the garden by the wood-shed. Perhaps they were there? But would they be bright and shining? No, they certainly wouldn't! Well, perhaps he would have a minute to rub them up before he took them in to Daddy and Uncle.

It was raining fast. Goodness, those tools would be dreadfully wet if he had left them out in the rain! Ah, there was the box, just inside the wood-shed! Perhaps he had put the tools inside, after all.

No, they were not there. The box was quite empty. Then Ian began to hunt for them all over the place. But, of course, it was no good hunting because Peeky the gnome had taken them off to his hollow tree, and at that very minute they were drying nicely all round his stove!

But Ian didn't know that. He thought they must be still somewhere about. So he hunted here and he hunted there, he looked in the grass, he searched under the hedge, he looked EVERYWHERE – but no, the tools were gone.

Ian was wet through, frightened and miserable. He didn't like to go back to Daddy and Uncle Peter. But he had to, of course, because they called him.

"Well, have you brought the tools, young man?" asked Uncle Peter.

"No, I haven't," said Ian, hanging his head. "I can't find them."

Well, you should have heard Daddy then! How he scolded Ian! How angry he was, and how ashamed of a little boy who didn't even know where his splendid new tools were.

"You can go straight upstairs to bed," he said. "And there you'll stay for the rest of the day. And unless those tools are found by Saturday you won't go to the circus with Uncle Peter, as he promised. You'll just stay at home instead."

Ian nearly cried. It was dreadful to be sent to bed in front of Uncle Peter, but he had to go. Mother was sorry about it, too, but she said that bed was the best place for boys who couldn't look after their things properly.

That was Wednesday. All day Thursday Ian hunted for

those tools and all day Friday. He couldn't find a single one of them, and when he went to bed on Friday night he was very miserable. He knew that Daddy wouldn't let him go to the circus the next day with Uncle Peter. Daddy always meant what he said.

What was happening to those tools? Ah, they were having a splendid time! They had made all the chairs, a most beautiful round table, a lovely deep cupboard, and the sturdiest little stool you ever saw for Peeky the gnome. They had enjoyed themselves tremendously, for there is nothing a good tool likes so much as doing a good job in a good workman's hands.

Peeky had looked after them carefully, and they looked as good as new. When all his furniture was finished on Friday night, and Tippy the elf had seen it, and clapped her hands for joy, Peeky spoke to the tools.

"Well, I suppose I'd better take you back?" he said. "What a pity! I have so loved using you – and now you'll have to go back to a nasty little boy who doesn't care what he does to you!"

"Peeky, couldn't you tell him to care for us better?" said the big saw, in its grating voice. "You'll have to tell him how you borrowed us, anyhow – so you could just as well tell him to keep us nicely."

"Very well, I will," said Peeky. "And what's more, I'll tell him that I'll come and take you away for good if he doesn't look after you properly! ha ha! that will make him sit up and take notice!"

Peeky put all the shining tools carefully into a big bag, and off he started for Ian's house. It was dark when he got there, and the nursery had no light in it. Peeky guessed that Ian was in bed. He climbed up the pear-tree outside the window and slipped into the room.

102

He was too surprised to speak

Ian was there, thinking sadly of the circus he wouldn't see the next day. Suddenly he heard a sound by the window, and he switched on his light. When he saw Peeky the gnome there, a big bag over his shoulder, he was too surprised to speak.

"Hallo, Ian," said Peeky. "I've brought back your tools. You left them out in the rain on Wednesday, poor things, so I took them home and dried them. Then I cleaned off the rust. They asked me to use them for some work I had to do, so I did. I kept them beautifully, as you see. Now I've brought them back because they're yours, but let me tell you this – if you don't look after them properly I shall come and take them away again – and you won't get them back next time! You're a careless little boy."

"I know," said Ian, looking ashamed. "Well, I *am* glad you've brought them back, little gnome. I missed them on Wednesday, and I've had a dreadful time trying to find them!"

He told the gnome all about it. Peeky listened.

"Well, it serves you right," he said. "It was a good punishment for you. Now, you'll remember what I say, won't you? You'll look after the tools properly?"

"Yes, I will," promised Ian. "And I'll look after *everything* properly – my books, my motor-car, and all my other toys. I'll be very careful in future. And please come and borrow my tools whenever you want to, little gnome. You'll always find them bright and shining!"

Ian took the tools to Daddy and Uncle the next day, and they were pleased to find them so bright and shining.

"Just in time, Ian!" said Daddy. "You can go to the circus now – but I really think it was careless of you to lose your tools for three days. Mind you don't do it again!"

Ian went happily off to the circus – but you may be sure

he had learnt his lesson. He looks after all his belongings VERY carefully now, especially his tools. When Peeky the gnome comes to borrow them, they are always clean and bright. I know because Peeky told me himself when he showed me a new book-case he had made for Tippy!

Dumble-Dee's Growing-Spell

Dumble-Dee was a most forgetful little pixie. His mother said he simply didn't *try* to remember what he was told. So, of course, when he went out to buy meat he came home with fish, and when he went out to buy cakes he came home with cigarettes. He simply could *not* remember what he was going to do.

One day he bought some seeds to plant in his garden, and wanted them to grow quickly. So he went to buy a growing-spell from the Tall Wizard.

"It's sixpence," said the Tall Wizard. "You just touch the seeds with this brush, Dumble-Dee, and they will grow as big and as fast as you like. I must tell you the word that stops them – it is "Apple-pie". Now just make a note of that – apple-pie – for you will want to use it."

"Oh, it's easy enough to remember apple-pie," said Dumble-Dee, and he went off with the growing-spell. He touched all his seeds with it and put them into his garden. They began to grow beautifully, and when they were as big as he wanted them to be, he stopped them.

"Apple-pie! " he said, and they stopped.

Now there was some of the growing-spell still left on the brush, but Dumble-Dee didn't know this. He got the brush out in a day or two and thought he would paint the wall where he had spilt some ink the week before. So he mixed his paint and took up his brush, but before he could dip his brush into the paint-box, Sooty the cat came along and rubbed himself against Dumble-Dee.

"Oh, go away, puss," said Dumble-Dee crossly, and he pushed the black cat away with his brush. Well, of course, there was still some growing-spell left there, and it worked! Dumble-Dee didn't notice the cat at first, but busied himself with washing the dirty spot on the wall. The cat came up to him again and rubbed himself hard against Dumble-Dee.

Dumble-Dee felt as though a tiger had pushed him, and he rolled over – bump! He looked round to see whatever had run into him, and he saw his cat! And how he stared, because Sooty was four times his right size! The growing-spell had made him grow at once, and he was still growing!

"Mercy me!" shouted Dumble-Dee in alarm. "What's happeneed to Sooty! Mother! Mother! Look at Sooty."

His mother came running in from the kitchen and stared in astonishment at the cat. Sooty ran over to her and tried to rub himself against her, but as he was now almost as big as Dumble-Dee's mother, the pooor woman was pushed over like a skittle! Down she went, and the cat tried to get on her lap!

"Dumble-Dee, what have you done to Sooty?" cried his mother. "You naughty pixie, what have you done?"

"Nothing at all," said Dumble-Dee indignantly, and then he suddenly thought of his brush. Could there have been any growing-spell left on it? There must have been!

"Oh, Mother!" he said. "I know what it is! I had some growing-spell left on my brush, and I touched Sooty with it when I pushed him away from me, and the magic is working and making him grow! Oh, Mother, what shall we do?"

"Do, silly? Why, say the word to stop him growing, of course!" cried his mother. "Do you want him to get as big as an elephant? See, he's as high as the grandfather clock already!"

Dumble-Dee opened his mouth to say the word, but he couldn't remember it! What could it be, oh, what could it be?

"It's something to eat!" he cried. "Yes, it's treacle pudding!"

The cat went on growing. "It's not treacle pudding," said his mother. "Quick, think again!"

"Plum-tart!" yelled Dumble-Dee. The cat went on growing. It put up its paw playfully and smacked Dumble-Dee. The pixie fell into the fender and felt as if he had been hit by a giant!

"Milk pudding!" he said, feebly. "Blancmange! Jam and rice! Raspberry jelly! Oh, Mother, it's something to eat. I know it is. What can it be?"

The cat went on growing. It reached the ceiling! Whatever would happen now? It couldn't possibly get out of the window, nor out of the door – it was much too big! What was that word, oh, what *was* it?

"Gingerbread! Blackberry pudding! Trifle! Chocolate buns!" shouted Dumble-Dee, trying to think of all the things there were to eat. The cat blinked its enormous green eyes at him, wondering why Dumble-Dee looked so small. And still it went on growing!

"It's growing through the ceiling!" groaned Dumble-Dee's mother. "Mind the plaster, Dumble-Dee – it's cracking and falling! Oh, what a silly you are! Do, do remember that word!"

The cat's head went through the ceiling up to the roof. It was surprised at itself. Whatever could be happening? It mewed, and its mew was so loud that all the mice for a mile around shivered in their shoes!

Crash! A chimney-pot fell off the roof, for the cat grew through the tiles! Its great head pushed through the roof, and it looked out through the hole, most astonished. As for everyone passing by, they stared as if they couldn't believe their eyes, and then they fled for their lives. They knew something queer was happening! A cat as large as a giant, poking its head through the roof – whatever next!

"Seed cake, sugar biscuits, shortbread, suet pudding, jam-roll, treacle tart!" shouted Dumble-Dee, but the cat went on growing! And goodness knows what would have happened if the Tall Wizard hadn't come by at that very moment, and, to his very great astonishment, seen a giant cat's head sticking out through the roof, getting larger every minute!

"Stars and moon, what's this?" said the Tall Wizard, in amazement. "Looks like a growing-spell gone wrong!"

He went to the door and peeped in. Most of the door-way was blocked by the cat's enormous furry tail, which was sticking out by the yard! "What's happening here?" cried the Wizard.

"Oh, is that you, Tall Wizard?" said Dumble-Dee's poor mother, who was squashed against the wall, almost choked with cat's fur. "Oh, do say the word to stop this cat growing. Dumble-Dee has forgotten it!"

"Apple-pie!" said the Wizard at once, and the cat stopped growing! "Apple-pie!" said the Wizard again, and the cat became smaller. Then the Wizard and Dumble-Dee's mother all shouted out the word together, "Apple-pie!"

And before long the cat was its own size again, very

'Stars and Moon, what's this?' said the Tall Wizard

much surprised, and there was a large hole in the roof, and two chimneys broken in the yard. Dear, dear!

"And now, Dumble-Dee," said his mother sharply, "you can go to the builder's yard and buy two new chimneys, some new tiles, and a rafter or two, and you can spend the rest of the week mending our cottage! That will perhaps teach you to remember things a bit better!"

So that is what Dumble-Dee is doing, and as it is very cold weather at the moment, he isn't at all enjoying himself sitting up on the roof with the east wind biting his nose! I wonder if his memory will be better now. The Tall Wizard says his brains want polishing, but I really don't know how that can be done, do you?

The Tooth Under The Pillow

George was very pleased because he had a loose tooth. It was right in the front, and whenever he bit anything the tooth wobbled about.

George liked it, but his mother didn't.

"It might get fixed into something you are eating, and then you will swallow it," she said to George. "Let me take hold of it and pull it out gently, George. It won't hurt you."

"Oh, I don't mind about it hurting," said George, who was a brave boy, and never cried even when he fell down and hurt both knees at once. "I *like* having a loose tooth, Mummy. I like it very much. It feels so nice when it wobbles."

"Well, darling, it worries me," said his mother. "Why don't you pull it out yourself, and put it under your pillow tonight? The fairies may come and get it, and leave you a sixpence in exchange."

"Oooh!" said George, and he went away to the garden to think about it. His money-box was full, so he didn't need the sixpence – what he was thinking about was the chance of seeing fairies!

You see, he had hunted for them all over the place – in the trees, in the bushes, in the flowers, in the nursery, even in the coal-hole. But he had never found one, not even a very small one. And now, here was Mummy saying that the fairies might actually come into his bedroom that night!

"Suppose I keep awake!" thought George. "Suppose I

111

saw them! I might follow them and see where they went! Oooh! That would be a most splendid adventure! I'll certainly pull my tooth out and put it under my pillow!"

So he went to his chest of drawers and took out a clean handkerchief. Then he leaned over and looked at his tooth in the glass. He wobbled it for the last time. It really was a fine tooth to wobble. Then he wrapped a corner of the handkerchief round it, and gave it a little jerk. It came out like a nut form its shell, and lay in his handkerchief, a dear little white tooth. There was a small hole in his mouth where the tooth had come from, but George knew that a grand new tooth would soon grow there.

He wrapped the tooth up in his handkerchief and took it to his mother. She was so pleased.

"You are really a very good little boy, George," she said, and kissed him. "I will put the tooth under your pillow tonight, and the fairies are sure to come and take it and leave you sixpence in exchange."

"Good!" said George, and went out to play with his tricycle.

That night George really felt most excited. He undressed and went to bed as usual. He said his prayers and snuggled down into bed. His mother slipped the little tooth under his pillow. George put up his hand and felt it there very small and hard. Then his mother kissed him good night and left him.

As soon as she was gone, George slipped out of bed and dressed himself again. You see, he didn't know where the fairies might lead him, and he didn't want to go out into the cold night with only his sleeping-suit on. He was really a very sensible little boy.

He got into bed again. He even had his shoes on, but he made sure that they were quite clean before he got into bed. Then he lay still and waited. He heard the clock strike eight – and nine – and ten – and then he began to get very sleepy indeed. His eyes kept closing themselves, and he had to prop them open with his fingers. Even then they closed on his fingers.

Eleven o'clock struck. George felt a little less sleepy, for he thought that the fairies would probably come at midnight, and he wouldn't have long to wait. He began to listen for them.

"Dong-dong-dong-dong," began the clock in the hall, striking twelve. "Dong-dong-dong-dong, dong-dong-dong-dong!"

"Midnight! George shut his eyes and pretended to be fast asleep. And just then he heard a noise! His heart beat fast! Someone was opening the door of his room. Someone crept up to his bed and slipped a hand under his pillow! Someone took away his tooth!

George's heart beat so loudly that he thought it must be heard all over the house! Whoever it was that had come into the room was now stealing away. Very quietly the little boy slipped out of bed and went to the door. He saw the Someone going down the stairs, a shadow in the darkness. He went downstairs, too. Out of the garden door went the Someone, and George went as well.

And then, when the Someone walked out into the moonlight, George saw what he was! The Someone was a gnome, with a curling beard, a high-pointed hat, and long, bony legs!

"So Mummy was right! The fairies *do* come and take our teeth if we put them under our pillows," said George to himself, most excited. "Now I must just see where this gnome goes, and then another day I can go there and see the fairies whenever I like!"

The gnome went down the garden-path and then, to George's enormous surprise, he saw that a small motor-car stood outside the gate! The gnome had come in that!

"R-r-r-r-r-r!" The gnome started up the engine of the car, and George ran forward, meaning to ask him a few questions. But the car was making such a noise that the gnome did not hear or see the little boy. George caught hold of the car and jumped on the running-board. The car started with a jerk, and off it went, with the gnome, and George, too!

The little boy climbed into the back of the car. This adventure was rather running away with him. He didn't like to tap the gnome on the shoulder in case it startled him and made him run into the ditch. So he just sat there at the back of the car and looked where he was going.

It was a most exciting ride. The gnome ran down the path that went through the wood, and then came to a part that was hung with bright lanterns. Fairies, elves, brownies, and gnomes ran about. George saw one party of them having a picnic with toadstools for tables. Then they came to a town that George thought must be Toy-town, for the houses were just like dolls' houses, and the trees stood on wooden stands and looked as if they could be knocked over at a touch.

On went the car through the night. At last it ran up a steep hill and stopped outside a little house that was brightly lighted inside. The gnome jumped out and turned to go up the path.

George called to him.

"I say! I hope you don't mind – but I came with you."

The gnome jumped so much that his hat fell off. He stared at George in astonishment.

114

"Snakes and ladders!" he said. "Where did you come from?"

"I'm the little boy whose tooth you took," said George. "I did so want to see a fairy, so I stayed awake."

"Well, well, well!" said the gnome, putting his hat on again. "I think you'd better go back home."

"Oh, no," said George, getting out of the car. "I do want to see what you do with my tooth. Please show me."

"Very well, come in and see," said the gnome. So the small boy went up the path with the gnome, and they both stepped inside the brightly lighted house. George looked round. He saw a cosy room, lit by a bright fire, and by it sat two other gnomes, both exactly like the first one.

"Good evening," they said, and they got up and bowed.

"Good evening," said George.

"This is the boy whose tooth I got this evening," said the first gnome. "He came after me. He's quite nice. Let's have some cocoa, shall we, and some chocolate biscuits? It isn't often we have a visitor."

"Certainly," said the other gnomes.

"My name is George," said George.

"And mine is Snip," said the first gnome, "and these are Snap and Snorum. We live here and do our work."

Soon a large jug of hot cocoa stood on the table, and a dish of the biggest chocolate biscuits that George had ever seen. Snip poured out three cups of cocoa.

"George wants to know what we do with the teeth we get," he said. "Shall we show him?"

"Yes," said Snap. He went to a cupboard in the wall and took out a big box. He took off the lid and set the box in front of George.

The little boy looked inside and exclaimed in delight. The box was full of the tiniest carved animals he had ever

It was a most exciting ride

seen! There were all kinds there – dogs, cats, horses, hens, goats, lions, tigers – a regular zoo! George picked some up. They were most beautifully carved.

"Put some out on the table," said Snorum, "and watch what happens."

George set out twelve of the tiny animals. Snorum scattered a fine yellow powder over them and blew softly, saying a very magic word under his breath. And, do you know, all those tiny carved animals came alive and ran about, prancing, jumping, kicking, as happy as could be!

"Oh!" said George, in delight. "I never in my life saw such a thing! Oh! What are they for?"

"We make them for the children of the fairy king and queen," said Snip. "They love them, you know. The queen has ordered a hundred for Christmas. The fairy princes and princesses are very tiny, and the toys that Father Christmas makes are far too big for them to play with. So we take the little ivory teeth that children don't want, and carve them for toys. We always pay for them, though."

"Yes, I know you do," said George. "You pay sixpence. My mother told me."

"I paid you a shilling tonight," said Snip. "I found I hadn't a sixpence, so I left a shilling under your pillow."

"Well, you can have my next tooth for nothing, then," said George. "Oh, I *am* pleased to know all this. I did so wonder what you wanted children's first teeth for. How pleased the little princes and princesses will be with these lovely animals!"

"We have done ninety-nine," said Snorum, blowing on the animals, and making them stop jumping and running about. "Your tooth will be carved by Snap, and make the hundredth. Then they will be packed into a beautiful box, and Snip will take them to the palace on Christmas Eve."

"Oh, how I wish I could see my tooth when it is made into a little carved animal," said George. "What animal will it be, Snap?"

"A bunny," said Snap. "That's the only animal we haven't carved so far."

"Oh, I *love* bunnies," said George. "They are my favourite animals."

"Look here, why shouldn't George come on Christmas Eve and see his tooth finished?" said Snip suddenly. "He is such a nice boy – so well behaved – and it would be nice for him to see his tooth when it is a little white rabbit. I could fetch him in our car quite easily."

"Oh, I say! That would be simply lovely!" cried George delighted. "Do, do come! I'll be ready!"

"Very well," said Snip, beaming at George. "I'll fetch you. Now, take a chocolate biscuit in your pocket and say good-bye. I'll run you back in my car."

Well, George was so sleepy in the car that his eyes closed, and he knew nothing of the ride back at all. Snip was very kind. He carried the little boy to his bedroom, undressed him, and put him to bed. Then he stole off.

In the morning George woke up and remembered everything. He felt under his pillow, and, sure enough, there was some money there. He pulled it out – a bright, new shilling!

"Oooh! That's just what Snip said," said George. "My, what a night I had! And I'm going again on Christmas Eve. I shall see my tooth made into a little ivory rabbit!"

Isn't he lucky? He keeps feeling his teeth to see if another one wobbles, because, you see, he owes Snip a tooth, and he thinks it would be so nice to give it to him on Christmas Eve! I'd love to go with him, wouldn't you?

If *you* have a loose tooth, you'll know what to do with it – and if you manage to keep awake, I hope you see Snip! But I rather think he'll be on the look-out for wide-awake girls and boys now!

The Magic Easter Egg

Once upon a time there was a brownie called Pop-up, who simply loved chocolate. He had chocolate biscuits for breakfast, chocolate pudding for dinner, chocolate cake for tea, and hot chocolate drink at night for his supper. It's a wonder he didn't turn into a chocolate himself!

Now one day he passed by Dame Shoo-hoo's house and saw her making a marvellous Easter egg. It was very big – bigger than Pop-up himself – and didn't it smell good!

Pop-up peeped in at the window and looked at it. How he longed to get a bite! Just one bite – a very little one! Nobody would notice one little bite in an egg so large as that!

Just as he was thinking this, Dame Shoo-hoo put on her bonnet and took up her basket to go shopping. Pop-up popped round to the back of her cottage as she went down the front path. When she had safely turned the corner the naughty little brownie slipped in at the back door and ran to look at the big Easter egg.

"Oooh! What a lovely one! I really must have a bite," said Pop-up – and he nibbled a bit off. It tasted so good that he bit off another piece – and another – and another, and do you know, very soon he had eaten quite a large hole in the Easter egg!

Suddenly he heard the sound of a door opening – it was Dame Shoo-hoo coming home again! Goodness! Now what was Pop-up to do? He knew quite well he would get a good spanking if Dame Shoo-hoo found him. In a fright he jumped through the hole he had made in the egg – and landed right in the very middle of the egg itself.

There he crouched, trembling, whilst Dame Shoo-hoo bustled about getting her tea. Suddenly she saw the hole in her beautiful egg and stood staring in horror.

"Who's been nibbling my fine egg?" she cried. "It must be that naughty dog from next door! He ate my sausages last week, and my biscuits yesterday, and now he's been in an nibbled my egg. I shall have to make some more chocolate to patch up the hole."

Dame Shoo-hoo was so sure that it was the dog who had eaten the chocolate that she didn't dream of looking inside. She made some more chocolate and patched up the hole. Soon poor Pop-up, inside the egg, was quite in the dark. He could see, smell, and feel nothing round him but dark chocolate. It was dreadful.

He did not dare to move. Once, by mistake, he slipped and sat down inside the egg! Bump! Dame Shoo-hoo looked round her room in surprise. "Did I hear a mouse?" she said. "Or was it soot falling down the chimney?"

Pop-up hardly dared to breathe. He sat inside the egg all that evening, and slept there for the night. It was really most uncomfortable. In the morning Dame Shoo-hoo put the egg in her barrow and wheeled it off to Mr. Feefo, who had ordered it from her for his children. Dame Shoo-hoo was surprised to find the egg so heavy.

"Dear me!" she said. "I must have put more chocolate in it than I thought I had. How peculiar!"

120

She wheeled it to Mr. Feefo's. He lifted it out of the barrow and put it into his study, where he mean to hide it till the time came for him to give it to his children.

It was so heavy that he rolled the great egg over and over down the passage to his study. Poor Pop-up inside was rolled over and over, too – bump-bump-bumpity-bump! Bump-bump-bumpity-bump!

Mr. Feefo left the egg in his study. Pop-up was frightened, because he knew Mr. Feefo would spank him much harder than Dame Shoo-hoo, if he found him inside the egg – and he certainly would be found the next morning when all the little Feefo children began to eat the egg.

What was he to do? Pop-up thought and thought – and he knew there was only one thing he could do. He must eat his way right out of the egg.

But, oh, dear! – he did so hate the thought of chocolate now. He had smelt it for hours, and felt it, too, and he thought he never wanted to see chocolate in his life again. But there was nothing else to be done. He must eat his way out. So he began.

Poor Pop-up, unfortunately, chose a place where the wall of the egg was extra thick. He licked it and licked it. He bit a bit off and chewed it up. He went on and on, and at last he felt he really couldn't eat a single bit more. So he had a rest, and then he heard Mr. Feefo come into the study.

"There must be a mouse or something in here," said the voice of Mr. Feefo. "I can distinctly hear a nibble-nibble-nibble!"

Pop-up stayed quite still inside the egg. After he had looked round, Mr. Feefo went out, puzzled. Then Pop-up did not dare to nibble or bite again. He just licked the chocolate, trying his hardest to make a hole so that he might get out.

Mr. Feefo's dog flew at Pop-up

He licked all day long – and at last, about ten o'clock that night, he had made a hole big enough to get his arm out. He put his hand out and broke away bits of egg round the edge of the hole. He must hurry, hurry, hurry, for he wanted to run home before Mr. Feefo locked up for the night.

The hole was big enough to jump out – Pop-up put out a leg – and then another – and out he jumped, covered with bits of chocolate and feeling very ill. He made his way softly into the hall – and just at that very minute Mr. Feefo's dog came along and saw him. He flew at Pop-up, who shot to the front door. He got out safely – but left behind part of his trousers in the dog's mouth! Poor Pop-up!

He got home and sat down trembling. Then he lit his fire and boiled up a big can of water. He meant to have a bath and wash away the dreadful smell of chocolate.

He didn't feel really safe till he was in bed. Tomorrow he would put a patch on his trousers, for they were the only ones he had. And never, never would he eat chocolate again! He was tired of the very smell of it.

"Nobody will ever know I was inside Feefo's egg," said Pop-up to himself, as he fell asleep. But he wouldn't have felt so happy about it if he had known that Mr. Feefo was watching out for somebody with patched trousers the next day.

Ah, Pop-up, what will happen to you then? You *will* get a shock!

ENID BLYTON is Dragon's bestselling author. Her books have sold millions of copies throughout the world and have delighted children of many nations. Here is a list of her books available in Dragon Books:

FIRST TERM AT MALORY TOWERS	50p	☐
SECOND TERM AT MALORY TOWERS	50p	☐
THIRD YEAR AT MALORY TOWERS	50p	☐
UPPER FOURTH AT MALORY TOWERS	50p	☐
IN THE FIFTH AT MALORY TOWERS	50p	☐
LAST TERM AT MALORY TOWERS	50p	☐
MALORY TOWERS GIFT SET	£2·55	☐
6 Books by Enid Blyton		

THE TWINS AT ST CLARE'S	50p	☐
SUMMER TERM AT ST CLARE'S	50p	☐
SECOND FORM AT ST CLARE'S	50p	☐
CLAUDINE AT ST CLARE'S	50p	☐
FIFTH FORMERS AT ST CLARE'S	50p	☐
THE O'SULLIVAN TWINS	50p	☐
ST CLARE'S GIFT SET	£2·55	☐
5 Books by Enid Blyton		

MYSTERY OF THE BANSHEE TOWERS	50p	☐
MYSTERY OF THE BURNT COTTAGE	50p	☐
MYSTERY OF THE DISAPPEARING CAT	50p	☐
MYSTERY OF THE HIDDEN HOUSE	50p	☐
MYSTERY OF HOLLY LANE	50p	☐
MYSTERY OF THE INVISIBLE THIEF	50p	☐
MYSTERY OF THE MISSING MAN	50p	☐
MYSTERY OF THE MISSING NECKLACE	50p	☐
MYSTERY OF THE PANTOMIME CAT	50p	☐
MYSTERY OF THE SECRET ROOM	50p	☐
MYSTERY OF THE SPITEFUL LETTERS	50p	☐
MYSTERY OF THE STRANGE BUNDLE	50p	☐
MYSTERY OF THE STRANGE MESSAGES	50p	☐
MYSTERY OF TALLY-HO COTTAGE	50p	☐
MYSTERY OF THE VANISHED PRINCE	50p	☐

CHILDREN'S LIFE OF CHRIST	30p	☐
THE BOY WHO TURNED INTO AN ENGINE	40p	☐
THE BOOK OF NAUGHTY CHILDREN	35p	☐
A SECOND BOOK OF NAUGHTY CHILDREN	35p	☐

PONY BOOKS are very popular with boys and girls.
Dragon Books have a fine selection by the best authors to choose from:

JUMP TO THE STARS	Gillian Baxter	50p	☐
THE DIFFICULT SUMMER	Gillian Baxter	50p	☐
THE PERFECT HORSE	Gillian Baxter	60p	☐
SUE'S CIRCUS HORSE	Judith Berrisford	50p	☐
PONIES ALL SUMMER	Judith Berrisford	50p	☐
PONY FOREST ADVENTURE	Judith Berrisford	50p	☐
TROUBLE AT PONYWAYS	Judith Berrisford	50p	☐
SILVER BRUMBY'S KINGDOM	Elyne Mitchell	50p	☐
SILVER BRUMBIES OF THE SOUTH	Elyne Mitchell	50p	☐
SILVER BRUMBY	Elyne Mitchell	50p	☐
SILVER BRUMBY'S DAUGHTER	Elyne Mitchell	50p	☐
MY FRIEND FLICKA PART 1	Mary O'Hara	60p	☐
MY FRIEND FLICKA PART 2	Mary O'Hara	60p	☐
GREEN GRASS OF WYOMING 1	Mary O'Hara	40p	☐
GREEN GRASS OF WYOMING 2	Mary O'Hara	40p	☐
GREEN GRASS OF WYOMING 3	Mary O'Hara	40p	☐
THUNDERHEAD 1	Mary O'Hara	40p	☐
THUNDERHEAD 2	Mary O'Hara	40p	☐
THUNDERHEAD 3	Mary O'Hara	40p	☐
FOR WANT OF A SADDLE	Christine Pullein-Thompson	50p	☐
IMPOSSIBLE HORSE	Christine Pullein-Thompson	35p	☐
THE SECOND MOUNT	Christine Pullein-Thompson	35p	☐
THE EMPTY FIELD	Christine Pullein-Thompson	50p	☐
THREE TO RIDE	Christine Pullein-Thompson	60p	☐
THE PONY DOPERS	Christine Pullein-Thompson	50p	☐
PONY PATROL	Christine Pullein-Thompson	40p	☐
PONY PATROL S.O.S.	Christine Pullein-Thompson	40p	☐
PONY PATROL FIGHTS BACK	Christine Pullein-Thompson	50p	☐

Outstanding fiction from the Dragon list.

INVISIBLE MAGIC   Elisabeth Beresford   60p ☐

What happens when a modern boy *half*-releases a centuries old spell.

DANGEROUS MAGIC   Elisabeth Beresford   60p ☐

Sammy and Eleanor pledge themselves to help the Unicorn get back to its own Place and Time. But where is that? And when?

THE BIG TEST   Roy Brown   50p ☐

A fast-moving adventure story set in the streets around London's Oval cricket ground on the last day of the Test.

A NAG CALLED WEDNESDAY   Roy Brown   50p ☐

When Liz and Larry 'find' a horse wandering the London streets, they think that keeping it will be easy. A funny and exciting chase story.

ROBIN HOOD   Antonia Fraser   40p ☐

The adventures of the fabulous hero in a stirring retelling.

NO PONIES FOR MISS POBJOY
          Ursula Moray Williams   50p ☐

The girls of Canterdown were mad on horses. Their new head-mistress cared only for cars – and for passing exams. A hilarious school story with a difference.

THE HOUSE IN CORNWALL   Noel Streatfield   35p ☐

A west country holiday with an unknown uncle could be fun. Or it could be dismal. Edward, Sorrell and Wish certainly were to find it surprising – and dangerous.

THE WINTER OF ENCHANTMENT
          Victoria Walker   20p ☐

A magic mirror transports Sebastian from his Victorian world of winter snow to the magic world of Melissa, Mantari and the wicked enchanter.

TEN-MINUTE TALES	50p ☐
TWENTY-MINUTE TALES	50p ☐
MORE TWENTY-MINUTE TALES	30p ☐
THE LAND OF FAR-BEYOND	35p ☐
BILLY-BOB TALES	35p ☐
TALES OF BETSY MAY	35p ☐
NAUGHTY AMELIA JANE	35p ☐
AMELIA JANE AGAIN	50p ☐
BIMBO AND TOPSY	50p ☐
EIGHT O'CLOCK TALES	35p ☐
THE YELLOW STORY BOOK	50p ☐
THE RED STORY BOOK	35p ☐
THE BLUE STORY BOOK	50p ☐
THE GREEN STORY BOOK	35p ☐
TRICKY THE GOBLIN	35p ☐
THE ADVENTURE OF BINKLE AND FLIP	50p ☐
THE ADVENTURES OF MR PINK-WHISTLE	35p ☐
MR PINK-WHISTLE INTERFERES	35p ☐
MR PINK-WHISTLE'S PARTY	50p ☐
MERRY MR MEDDLE	35p ☐
MR MEDDLE'S MUDDLES	35p ☐
MR MEDDLE'S MISCHIEF	40p ☐
DON'T BE SILLY MR TWIDDLE	50p ☐
ADVENTURES OF THE WISHING CHAIR	50p ☐

All these books are available at your local bookshop or newsagent, or can be ordered direct from the publisher. Just tick the titles you want and fill in the form below.

Name ....

Address ....

....

Write to Dragon Cash Sales, PO Box 11, Falmouth, Cornwall TR10 9EN. Please enclose remittance to the value of the cover price plus: UK: 22p for the first book plus 10p per copy for each additional book ordered to a maximum charge of 82p. BFPO and EIRE: 22p for the first book plus 10p per copy for the next 6 books, thereafter 3p per book. OVERSEAS: 30p for the first book and 10p for each additional book. *Granada Publishing reserve the right to show new retail prices on covers, which may differ from those previously advertised in the text or elsewhere.*